TEDDY JO

and the Strangers in the Pink House

TEDDY JO

AND THE
Strangers in the Pink House

HILDA STAHL

WindRider BOOKS
Tyndale House Publishers, Inc., Wheaton, Illinois

Dedicated with love to
Curtis, Ruth Ellen, Steve,
Kevin, and Craig Butler

Cover illustration by Gail Owens

Juvenile trade paper edition

Library of Congress Catalog Card Number 89-51920
ISBN 0-8423-6976-7
Copyright © 1982 by Hilda Stahl
All rights reserved
Printed in the United States of America

95 94 93 92 91 90
 8   7   6   5   4   3   2   1

Contents

1. Mom

Teddy Jo gently touched her flushed cheek and her blue eyes sparkled with pleasure. Mike's mom had kissed her! She really had! She'd smiled, then leaned down and kissed Teddy Jo right on the cheek.

Teddy Jo's heart almost burst through her stained tee shirt as she leaned against the bathroom counter and looked into the sparkling mirror. Did the kiss show at all? If someone looked at her would they say, "Hey, I see a kiss on your cheek"?

Suddenly the bathroom door opened and Teddy Jo whirled around. Mom stood there and she frowned impatiently at Teddy Jo.

"What's taking you so long in here, Theodora Josephine?" asked Carol as she reached for the curling iron. "I have to do my hair yet."

Teddy Jo backed to the door and stood with her thin shoulder pressed tightly against the door jamb. Maybe if she was really quiet she could watch Mom curl her hair. Maybe Mom would smile at her, then kiss her cheek. What would it feel like for Mom to kiss her? She gently touched her face. But maybe Mom didn't know how to kiss anyone except Dad.

"What're you staring at?" asked Carol sharply. "Haven't you seen anyone curl her hair before?" As she turned her head the white cord twisted and she impatiently straightened it. "You're making me nervous, Teddy Jo. Go find something to do with yourself."

Teddy Jo's cheeks grew hot and she backed out into the hall, then ran to her yellow and white room and slammed the door hard. "I'll bet Mike's mom would let me watch her curl her hair." Teddy Jo crossed her thin arms over her thin chest and stuck out her bottom lip in a pout. Mike's mom was always nice. She didn't yell or have to leave for work early every morning so that Mike and his brother were forced to get their own breakfast and lunch, and she usually stayed home at night unless the whole family went out together.

With a sigh Teddy Jo walked to her bed and sank down on the edge of it. The late afternoon sun still warmed her room and smells of summer drifted through the open windows. TV sounds from the living room blocked out any of the outdoor noises.

She twisted her toe in her gold carpet and rubbed her hands on her bare legs. Mom had hugged her once—last summer just after she'd told her about becoming a Christian. Maybe Mom would never hug her again.

Slowly she walked to the long mirror on her closet door. She scowled as she stood with her feet apart, her hands on her thin hips. Her long dark hair tangled around her narrow face. Catsup and mustard stains streaked the front of her yellow tee shirt. She scratched at them and wished she hadn't eaten that hot dog yesterday. She touched the hole in her blue shorts and wrinkled her small nose. She really was ugly. No wonder Mom couldn't stand to kiss her or hug her or talk nice to her. She frowned thoughtfully. Grandpa didn't think she was ugly.

He'd said, "You're my pretty little girl, Teddy Bear Jo."

She nodded hard with her lips pressed tightly together. Grandpa loved her. He liked to hug and kiss her. And he liked to have her hug and kiss him. She grinned sheepishly and ducked her head. Once she'd hated Grandpa. She'd hated everyone! Mom and Dad had broken up and sent her to live with Grandpa. Oh, but she'd hated that! Then one day after she'd lived with him awhile, she'd learned to love him and love God as her heavenly Father. And she'd learned to love her little brother, Paul, even if he did always wet his pants and smell like the restrooms at the park.

She looked around her beautiful room. She

lived with Mom and Dad and Linda and Paul
in their very own house in Middle Lake.
Thanks to Grandpa they didn't have to live in
dirty, run-down houses now. He'd sold some of
his precious black walnut trees and he'd bought
this house for them just because he loved
them.

Teddy Jo hugged herself and twirled around
the room. She loved this house, but she loved
Grandpa's place just as much. He lived outside
of town and she visited him often. They often
walked together through the acres and acres of
trees. She loved to swing on the tire swing
that he'd made for her on a fat maple branch
where Mom had once had a tire swing.

Abruptly Teddy Jo stopped at the window
and stared out at the soft green grass and red
roses and a robin on the branch of an oak tree.

Why didn't Mom love her? She didn't
scream and throw fits or punch people anymore. She was practically one of the nicest girls
around now. Why, she was so nice that she
hadn't even yelled at Linda yesterday when
she'd spilled perfume on Teddy Jo's gold
carpet.

Teddy Jo wrinkled her nose and looked at
the small stain on her carpet. She could've
yelled at Linda for daring to bring perfume into
her bedroom, but she hadn't. Linda knew she
didn't like perfume. *Yes*, Teddy Jo thought,
I'm pretty nice all right. Maybe she should
march right down the hall to the bathroom and

tell Mom just how nice she was! It might make a big difference.

She jerked open the door and Paul fell into the room. She stared at him in surprise, then anger. "Were you spying on me, Paul?"

He pushed himself up and sat cross-legged on the floor. His blue eyes looked big in his pale little face. Slowly he shook his head. "I wouldn't do that, Teddy Jo."

She pushed the door shut and leaned against it, her arms crossed, her lips pressed tightly together as she stared down at him.

He trembled. "Honest, Teddy Jo." He pulled himself into a little knot and watched her fearfully. "You won't hit me, will you?"

No way would she hit him! He ought to know that by now. She was a Christian and so was he, and he knew Christians didn't go around beating up their little brothers.

"You're scaring me, Teddy Jo," he whispered hoarsely.

She pushed away from the door and walked over and plopped down on her bed. No way would she scare him and have him wet her carpet and make her room stink. He twisted around to face her and she sighed and shook her head. "I'm not gonna hit you, Paul. Have I hit you lately? Have I?"

He swallowed hard and finally shook his head. "But you said you might if I didn't quit wetting my pants."

"And don't you forget it! But I wouldn't hit

you for any other reason that I can think of right now."

He rubbed the carpet. His hair was standing on end even though Grandpa had combed it very carefully this morning before Sunday school. His shorts and tee shirt hung on his lean body and one leg was scratched from thigh to knee. He bit his bottom lip then said, "Don't let Linda send me to bed early, Teddy Jo."

"Don't pay any attention to her. She thinks she's some kind of hot-shot now that she's thirteen."

"She said since she's baby-sitting tonight, I have to do what she says. She says I have to go to bed at six and I don't want to! I want to watch TV."

"Tell Mom or Dad."

Paul shook his head hard. "They would get mad."

Teddy Jo sighed. Paul was right. They didn't want to be bothered with such things as early bedtimes when they were going out for supper and a movie. "I'll take care of Linda."

Paul smiled and part of the color came back into his cheeks. "Can I watch TV?"

She grinned. "Sure. Why not? But not if something comes on that's bad for you. You know what Grandpa said."

"I won't watch anything that would make my mind dirty." Paul pushed himself up. "What would make my mind dirty?"

Teddy Jo's dark brows drew down in a

14

thoughtful frown. "I don't know. But if something comes on that would, you can't watch. We can call Grandpa and ask him if we're not sure."

He nodded. "All right."

Teddy Jo opened her door and motioned him out. She hesitated, then followed him down the hall to the living room, where the TV blared loudly. She frowned a warning at Paul to keep quiet while Dad watched TV. Paul sidled into the room and sat in a corner where he'd left a Matchbox car. Teddy Jo stopped at the wide front window and looked out at the sidewalk where Mike Brent stood talking to Marsha Wyman. Teddy Jo wrinkled her nose. How could Mike stand to talk to Marsha? Maybe they were getting a soccer game together. Maybe she should run out to see, so she could go to the park and play with them. She barely shook her head. She had to stay home since Mom and Dad were going out. Grandpa had told her to and she'd agreed.

"I'm ready, Larry," said Carol, and Teddy Jo turned around. Carol was dressed in white slacks and a pale apricot blouse and she looked very pretty. Her perfume stung Teddy Jo's nose, but Larry sniffed and smiled.

"You look as good as you smell," said Larry as he jumped up.

"We're going, Linda," called Carol.

Linda poked her head out of the kitchen. "Have fun tonight."

"We will," said Carol as she took Larry's arm.

They walked out the door and Teddy Jo stood at the window and watched them until they drove away. Did they even know that they had a girl named Teddy Jo Miller? Did they know that she was going to be eleven years old in one week? If she didn't know better, she'd think that she was adopted just like Cathy Norton from next door.

Finally Teddy Jo turned away from the window and walked to the couch and plopped down in the corner. She grabbed a blue throw pillow and held it tightly. She might as well watch TV with Paul and Linda. Too bad Grandpa wasn't here. Maybe they'd play Monopoly or he'd tell them stories about when he was a boy growing up in the country near Middle Lake.

She sighed and pulled her bony knees up to her chin. When she grew up and had a little girl of her own, she'd sit on the couch with her and never forget who she was. She'd let her little girl watch her curl her hair and she'd kiss and hug her all day long.

2. Making Plans

"When are you going to brush your hair, Teddy Jo?"

"When I feel like it, Linda. Not everyone wants to spend hours in front of the mirror just to brush long dark hair."

"You should enroll in night school to learn how." Linda impatiently turned back to watch TV and Teddy Jo took a deep breath to calm her hurt and anger. So what if she didn't always remember to brush her hair? Whom was she hurting? Who needed to have brushed hair just to sit and watch TV? Mom sure never noticed if her hair was brushed or not.

She bit her bottom lip and leaned her chin on her knees and tried to concentrate on the story on TV. Paul laughed along with the canned laughter, then turned with a flush and shot a look at Linda, then at Teddy Jo. When they didn't object, he laughed again, only softer.

17

Linda breathed deeply and locked her fingers together. How had she been born into this family? Teddy Jo was a slob and Paul a big baby who cried if you looked at him wrong. She should've been born into a rich family as an only child. It was embarrassing to admit to her friends that Teddy Jo was her sister. She wasn't as bad as she used to be, but she still wasn't all that great. They should've left her to live with Grandpa forever instead of just last summer. *He* thought Teddy Jo was wonderful.

Teddy Jo saw the scowl on Linda's face. Teddy Jo sat up straighter and lifted her chin a little. Couldn't she do or say anything to please Linda?

The doorbell rang and Teddy Jo shot out of her seat before Linda or Paul could move. Maybe it was Grandpa. It just had to be Grandpa!

Her heart leaped as she flung wide the door. The smile faded when she saw Cathy Norton.

"Oh, hi, Cathy. What do you want?"

Cathy laughed and flipped back her blonde hair as she stepped inside. "Boy, you really make me feel wanted, Teddy Jo."

"Sorry. I thought you were Grandpa."

"No. He's taller and heavier than I am."

Teddy Jo laughed and Linda scowled at her and told her to keep quiet. "Let's go to my room," Teddy Jo whispered, rolling her eyes and motioning toward Linda.

In the bedroom Cathy whirled around to

face Teddy Jo. "I came to help you plan your birthday party."

"My birthday party?"

"Sure. Don't you want to have one?"

Teddy Jo swallowed hard. "I've never had one before."

"Well, I have and I know what to do at birthday parties, so I came to help you plan yours." Her blue eyes sparkled. She was dressed in red shorts and a red plaid suntop. "I will be your first guest. Get a paper and pencil and we'll talk about who to invite and who not to."

"Mom will never let me have a party." Excitement bubbled inside Teddy Jo, but she refused to let it out.

"We'll plan it, then you show your plans to your mom and see what she says. Tell her that you'll do all the work and have the party in the backyard. I'll bet she says yes." Cathy plopped down on the bed and bounced happily. "We'll have so much fun!"

Teddy Jo stood very still, then twirled around with a glad shout. She would have a party! Maybe she'd get presents and everything! But what if nobody wanted to come to a party for Teddy Jo Miller? What if nobody cared that she'd be eleven years old on July 23?

Her heart sank and she dropped to the chair near her desk. She moved aside the paints and canvas and picked up a piece of lined paper and a stubby red pencil with a chewed-off

eraser. She'd plan with Cathy but she'd keep
her excitement down until Mom decided if she
could have a party or not. "I want balloons,"
she said as she printed *baaloones*. She looked
at the word with a frown, then shrugged. Who
cared how it was spelled? She knew what she
meant.

"My mom said she'd help us bake a birthday
cake," said Cathy as she hugged the rag doll
that leaned against the head of Teddy Jo's
white bed. "She said we could decorate it with
flowers and candles."

Teddy Jo closed her eyes and thought about
the cake and drew a picture of it in her mind.
Her eyes snapped open and with quick, deft
lines she drew a cake just the way she wanted
hers to be. She laughed and held it out to
Cathy.

"It looks real," said Cathy in awe. "I wish I
could draw the way you do."

Teddy Jo flushed with pleasure. She knew
she was a good artist, but she liked to have
others say so. Someday she'd be a famous artist
and everyone would buy her paintings for lots
of money—maybe as much as twenty dollars a
picture! Maybe even Mom and Dad would
want one of her pictures to hang in the living
room so they could tell everyone that their
daughter Teddy Jo had painted it.

She looked down at her hands with a frown.
Mom and Dad wouldn't even look at her art
work. They had actually crumpled up some of

her drawings and tossed them in the garbage! No, they sure didn't care about her art. They'd probably never care.

She smoothed out the lined paper and gripped the stubby pencil. "What shall I write, Cathy?"

Cathy pushed herself off the bed and stood beside Teddy Jo, frowning in concentration. "You spelled balloons wrong."

Teddy Jo shrugged as she forced back a blush. "Who cares? What else shall I put? I sure don't want any of those dumb party hats like I saw in Ben Franklin's. But birthday napkins with paper plates to go with them would sure be pretty." She'd never had plates and napkins that matched.

"Candy," said Cathy with a firm shake of her head. "You've got to have lots of candy so there's enough for everyone. I like butterscotch the best. And so does Dara Cook."

"I like it, too, so we'll get lots of butterscotch. And candy corn. I like that a lot."

"And M & M's with and without peanuts. They melt in your mouth, not in your hand." Cathy laughed as she held out her hands as if she was checking on melted chocolate.

They talked and planned and Teddy Jo wrote a guest list. Excitement churned inside her and burst out of her and she could barely sit still. She'd have the best birthday party in the whole world! She'd ask Grandpa to come or maybe she'd have the party at Grandpa's place so all the kids could swing on the tire swing and shout like cowboys. She laughed right out loud, then stopped when she saw that Cathy wasn't laughing.

"I just remembered something," said Cathy in a hushed voice. She sank to the edge of the bed and looked very mysterious. "Someone moved into the little pink house down the street."

"Who?" A strange little shiver ran down Teddy Jo's back.

"I don't know who. I saw the moving van and some of the furniture. Maybe tomorrow we can find out who moved in. We could stop on the way to the park. Maybe there'll be kids our age."

"Maybe." Teddy Jo walked across the room. For some reason she didn't want to find out who lived in the pink house. But that was silly. Maybe she'd meet a new friend, maybe even someone who liked art as much as she did.

Cathy looked around the bedroom and sniffed, then shook her head. "Your room smells funny."

"It does not! It smells like oil paints and fresh air. You should smell Linda's room. It stinks!" Teddy Jo wrinkled her nose. "It smells like powder and makeup and perfume. It makes me throw up just to walk into it."

"My mom let me try on her makeup." Cathy giggled. "I put blue stuff on my eyes. I sure looked funny."

Teddy Jo picked up the lined paper. "What if Marsha Wyman comes to the party—even if I don't invite her?"

"We'll just tell her to go home. She makes too much trouble all the time."

"I know." Teddy Jo thought of all the times in school that Marsha fought with her, mostly about soccer. Since Marsha lived right across the street it would be very easy for her to see the party and just walk over and join in. It might be fun to kick her out.

"Will you ask your mom tonight about your party?"

Teddy Jo's stomach knotted. "No. They'll get home too late and then go to work too early, so I'll ask her tomorrow afternoon. *If* she's not too tired."

Cathy nodded, then brightened. "I know! If your mom won't let you, then you can have it at my house. My mom loves to give birthday parties."

Teddy Jo smiled. No matter what, she was going to have a birthday party! Oh, she couldn't wait!

3. Strangers in the Pink House

"Will you hurry up, Paul?" Teddy Jo stood near the sink with her fists on her hips, glaring at Paul as he slowly ate his Cheerios. "I want to go to the park right now!"

Paul shivered and pushed back his plastic bowl. "I'm ready." He jumped up and twisted his shorts on his thin body.

Teddy Jo frowned and pushed him back to his chair. "Finish your Cheerios first. But hurry up!"

He sank down and pulled the bowl to himself and took a large bite, milk dripping down his chin, his fearful eyes on Teddy Jo.

She whirled around and looked out the window and saw Mike and his mother in their yard. "I'll wait outdoors for you, Paul." She dashed out, her heart racing. Maybe Jane Brent would kiss her again today. Her skin tingled just thinking about it.

The morning sun warmed Teddy Jo instantly and she quickly stepped in the shade of the

25

house beside Mike and Jane Brent. "Good morning," Teddy Jo said with a big smile.

"It's a beautiful day today, isn't it?" Jane smiled down at Teddy Jo. "Mike and I are going to the beach today. Todd's canoeing with friends of his. This is a beautiful day to play in the sun. What are your plans?"

"Paul and I are going to play at the park and maybe Grandpa will come over later." Teddy Jo wanted Jane Brent to invite them to go to the beach as she had many times in the past. It sure would feel good to bob under cool water and kick around and splash. She knew she could be ready in two minutes if Paul ever finished his Cheerios. But Jane Brent and Mike talked to her about everything else and didn't once say they wanted her to go with them. Finally Mike and his mom walked to their car and drove away, and Teddy Jo stood in the yard and watched until the small red car was out of sight. Her shoulders drooped and she listlessly tucked her tangled hair behind her ears. Mrs. Brent probably didn't care one bit about her.

Paul slammed the door and called, "I'm ready to go."

Teddy Jo stomped toward the sidewalk and Paul ran to catch up with her. He looked at her and knew by her face that he better not say one word or she'd be on him fast.

"Nobody ever wants to take us swimming," she muttered.

"I can swim," said Paul brightly.

"You can't either, so don't say you can."

Paul clamped his mouth shut. He didn't dare argue with Teddy Jo when she was acting this way. And he *could* swim. When they'd gone to the pool the last time, his feet had almost left the bottom when he paddled real hard with his hands and arms. She sure couldn't tell him he couldn't swim. Next time they went, he'd prove he could and then she wouldn't argue about it with him. Maybe she'd even say, "I was sure wrong, Paul. You can swim like a world champion. Well, I bet you could win a gold medal if you competed."

Teddy Jo stopped and pretended to tie her shoe, then she peeked at the pink house. A small brown car stood in the drive and a ten-speed bike leaned against the side of the house.

"Why're you staring at the pink house, Teddy Jo?"

She jumped up, her face red. "Who says I am?"

"Jim told me somebody moved in. I wonder if they've got a seven-year-old boy."

Inside the house a dog barked and Paul laughed. He wanted a dog of his own, but Mom and Dad said no dog would live in their new house and ruin their carpets.

"They've got a dog," whispered Teddy Jo, who wanted a dog as much as Paul did.

"Let's go ask them who they are and if we can see their dog."

Teddy Jo frowned down at him so hard that

he paled and shrank back. "We're going to the park right now. Let's go!" She ran down Oak Street and Paul followed. She knew he couldn't keep up and finally she slowed so he could catch up to her. His face was red and she knew hers was, too. She lifted her damp hair off her neck, then let it fall again.

At the park boys and girls shouted and played. Nobody was playing soccer so she couldn't join in for a fast, hard game. Dara Cook was there with her twin brothers. She waved and Teddy Jo waved back. Paul ran off to the slide where two other boys were playing. Teddy Jo stopped by the roses and smelled them and wished she could paint them. She tugged her green tee shirt over her ragged cutoffs. Her feet felt sweaty inside her tennis shoes. Suddenly she gave a loud whoop and ran toward the giant slide. She sped up the ladder, then flopped down and swooshed down to land in the sand below. Her legs stung and she rubbed them as she ran around to climb up again. At the top she stopped and clutched the hot metal and looked across the park. A woman and a girl about her size walked across the grass with a golden cocker spaniel on a leash. Teddy Jo hadn't seen them before. Maybe the woman was someone's grandmother.

Suddenly the dog tugged free and ran away, barking loudly.

28

"Come back, Honey," the girl shouted as she raced after the dog.

Teddy Jo pushed down the slide and plopped at the bottom and took off after the runaway dog at a dead run. Her hair blew back from her hot face and her blue eyes sparkled with excitement. This was better than a soccer game. Well, almost as good.

Paul saw the dog and he shouted and ran after it, too, his thin legs pumping up and down.

"Honey, come back!" shouted the woman as she ran after the girl.

Teddy Jo stopped and stared and blinked her eyes. She had never ever seen an old woman run. She was at least as old as Grandpa and she was running as fast as the girl!

Suddenly the dog stopped and dropped to the grass, panting hard. The girl dropped down beside it, then the woman. Paul skidded to a stop and stumbled and fell almost in the woman's lap. She laughed and Paul flushed with embarrassment.

"I tried to catch your dog," he said, pushing himself up.

Teddy Jo walked slowly to them and looked down at the dog and the people around it. "Is your dog all right?"

The woman nodded. "Honey is just fine. Thanks for trying to help us."

"Do you live near here?" asked the girl.

"At 712 Oak Street. I'm Teddy Jo Miller and this is my brother, Paul."

"I told you we'd find someone my age here, Grandma," said the girl excitedly. She had carrot-red hair and light brown eyes. She looked up at Teddy Jo with a happy laugh. "I'm Kandy Kane." She laughed again, then spelled it and Teddy Jo knew she'd die if she had a name like that that everyone would tease her about. "And this is my grandma, Anna Sloan. We live in the pink house on Oak Street."

"We knew somebody moved in," said Paul as he stroked the dog.

Mrs. Sloan pushed herself up. She was short and slightly plump with twinkling blue-green eyes and brown hair streaked with gray. She rubbed grass off her red slacks and pulled her knit top down in place. "Kandy and I are glad to find friends so soon. Honey did us a favor by running away from us, didn't she?"

Honey lifted her head and barked one short bark, then wriggled until her chin rested on Paul's bare leg. He looked ready to burst with happiness.

"Do you jog, Teddy Jo?" asked Kandy, flicking back her shoulder-length red hair. Her face and arms were covered with freckles.

"I guess so," said Teddy Jo with a shrug.

"We jog every day," said Anna Sloan. "Would you and Paul like to join us now? Maybe afterwards we can go to my place for something cold to drink."

30

Teddy Jo hesitated, then nodded. She fell into step beside Kandy and Mrs. Sloan jogged beside Paul, who held Honey's leash. Teddy Jo glanced at Kandy and back at Mrs. Sloan and decided they were very nice. Usually she didn't talk to strangers, but these strangers lived on her street in the pink house. They had to be all right to talk to and visit with.

"I'm going into fifth grade," said Kandy later as they walked down Oak Street.

"Me, too," said Teddy Jo. She didn't want to say that she was almost eleven and that really she should be going into sixth grade. She hated to have anyone know that she'd flunked second grade. But worse still she hated to have anyone know that she still read second-grade-level readers.

"Kandy goes to school in Port Huron, so she'll be going home to her parents in August," said Mrs. Sloan. "I'm going to miss her a lot, but it'll be nice to have young friends who remind me of her." She smiled right at Teddy Jo.

"Did you used to live in Grand Rapids?" asked Teddy Jo.

Anna Sloan shook her head. "Flint. But I drove through Middle Lake once on my way to Grand Rapids and I said that someday I'd like to live in such a quiet, pretty little town. So, here I am."

They stopped outside the pink house and Teddy Jo was just ready to walk in when she saw Cathy Norton waving to her from across the street. Cathy motioned urgently to her. Teddy Jo frowned, then said, "I'll see what she wants, then be right back."

"Invite her in, too," said Mrs. Sloan as she held the door wide for Paul and Honey.

"I will," said Teddy Jo. She ran to Cathy with a frown. "What do you want? We were ready to have cold orange juice. And I'm thirsty. She said you could come in with me."

Cathy shook her head, her eyes wide in alarm. She clutched Teddy Jo's arm. "Don't go in there," she whispered urgently. "Mom said that there's something strange about that woman. I think something terrible will happen to anyone who walks into that house."

"You're crazy." A shiver ran down Teddy Jo's back.

"No! Mom said she'd read something about that lady. You'd better get Paul out of there right now before something terrible happens to him."

Teddy Jo's mouth went dry and she tried to swallow. Cathy was making all this up for some crazy joke. Wasn't she?

4. Teddy Jo to the Rescue

"What will you do?" whispered Cathy hoarsely as they stared up the sidewalk that led to the pink house.

Teddy Jo swallowed hard. "I'll just go right in and get Paul and go home."

"What if she won't ever let you out of the house? What if she holds you in there and never lets you go? I saw a movie on TV about that." She clutched at Teddy Jo's sun-darkened arm. "Don't go in there!"

"I've got to. Paul's in there."

"Just stand at the door and call him out."

"He won't come if he's with the dog." Teddy Jo scowled impatiently. "Why am I listening to you? You don't know anything about Mrs. Sloan."

Cathy's blue eyes snapped and she flipped back her blonde hair. "Well, you go right in that house and see if I care if you come back out or not!"

"Well, I'm going to do just that!"

"Good!"

Teddy Jo marched right up to the door, her chin high and her back stiff. Cathy sure wasn't going to scare her out of going into the pink house for a glass of cold orange juice and maybe a chance to play with Honey.

"I might never see you again," called Cathy angrily. "If I don't, don't blame me!"

Teddy Jo looked over her thin shoulder at Cathy and made a face, then pushed the doorbell. Her stomach fluttered nervously but she sure didn't want Cathy to know it.

Kandy opened the door and Teddy Jo walked in without another glance at Cathy.

"Come into the kitchen," said Kandy. "Grandma even made rolls for us. She put them in the microwave so they're done already."

"Where's Paul?" asked Teddy Jo sharply as she looked around the small room. The smell of fresh baked rolls came from the kitchen.

"He's in the basement with Honey. He said he'd come up when we call him."

Teddy Jo hesitated outside the kitchen, then walked in and Anna Sloan turned from the counter where she was glazing the rolls. She smiled brightly and Teddy Jo managed a nervous grin.

"I hope you're hungry enough for a roll," Anna said. "Paul said he was."

Teddy Jo darted looks around the kitchen,

34

but nothing seemed sinister, so she relaxed a little. "I could eat a roll."

"Call Paul, Kandy." Anna motioned toward the table. "Teddy Jo, have a seat after you wash your hands."

She washed at the kitchen sink. Yellow gingham curtains fluttered at the open window and bright yellow tile with white daisies covered the wall around the sink and cupboards. She dried her hands on a yellow flowered towel that felt soft and looked new. Just as she sat at the table Paul stumbled into the room with Honey close behind him. Kandy pushed Honey back and closed the basement door. The dog whimpered a minute, then padded down the steps.

Anna set the plate of rolls in the center of the table, and put a glass of orange juice at each person's place. Teddy Jo reached for a roll and licked the glaze off. It was sweet and delicious. The roll was warm and yeasty and Teddy Jo suddenly felt as if she could eat ten of them.

Paul wolfed down his roll as Anna talked about Flint and Port Huron and how she and Kandy often had fished in Lake Huron for walleye and perch.

"I like to go fishing," said Paul around his roll. Teddy Jo frowned at him, but he kept talking. "Grandpa took me fishing and I caught a bass and a sunfish but they were too little to keep so I tossed them back. Grandpa caught some big ones and he cooked them and we ate them and I had to be careful of the bones."

Teddy Jo couldn't believe that Paul could talk so much. Usually he didn't make a peep around strangers. It had to be the dog. Or maybe Mrs. Sloan had done something to Paul to make him talk and talk and talk.

Teddy Jo choked and coughed and Kandy patted her back and asked if she was all right. Teddy Jo nodded, but wished she could get hold of Cathy right now and shake her hard for making up stories to scare her. There was nothing wrong with Mrs. Sloan or Kandy.

"Have you lived in Middle Lake all your life?" asked Anna as she leaned toward Teddy Jo.

"No." She couldn't tell about the terrible places she'd lived because Dad had been without work, then without unemployment checks.

"We moved here last summer," said Paul. "Grandpa bought our house for us."

"Does he live with you?" asked Kandy. She'd tried often to get Grandma to live with them, but she said she needed her privacy.

"He has a house out in the country," answered Teddy Jo.

"Do you have a grandma, too?" asked Kandy.

"Just a grandpa," said Paul. "He's nice."

Kandy remembered her grandpa. He'd been nice, too, but he'd gone to heaven to live with

36

Jesus three years ago when she was seven. She could still remember his reddish gray hair and booming laugh.

Just then the phone rang and Anna jumped up to answer it. She leaned against the counter near the back door and talked. Teddy Jo watched her face turn from a smile to a frown.

"You have to leave it that way, Arlo," snapped Anna. "I want him dead. No! I mean it!"

Teddy Jo gulped and chills ran over her body. What was Mrs. Sloan saying? Teddy Jo gripped her juice glass. Had she heard right?

Anna glanced at the table and caught Teddy Jo's eye, then turned her back and said in a low voice, "I must lay the phone down and get it in the study, Arlo."

Teddy Jo shivered and looked quickly at Kandy, but she was busy talking to Paul about fishing.

"Kandy, please hang the phone up when I pick it up in the study." Anna hurried out of the room, a worried frown on her face.

Teddy Jo jumped up and grabbed Paul and jerked him off his chair. "We have to go right now. Good-bye."

"I want to stay," wailed Paul, pulling back.

"You are coming with me," said Teddy Jo through her clenched teeth. She had to get Paul out before Mrs. Sloan came back and forced them to stay.

Paul wanted to jerk away from Teddy Jo but

he didn't dare. He knew she'd knock him right down and drag him out. Why in the world was she so anxious to leave? Why was she afraid? He wanted to ask her, but he clamped his mouth closed and didn't speak even when Kandy said good-bye and said she'd see them in the park sometime.

The sun was in his eyes outdoors and he blinked and finally Teddy Jo set him free. Paul rubbed his arm and tried to tell her that he was mad. But he couldn't do that and he knew it. Why fool himself? He didn't have the guts to speak up to anyone and least of all to Teddy Jo.

"We are never going back to that pink house," said Teddy Jo as she marched along the sidewalk toward their house. "And don't you dare try to sneak over there by yourself, Paul Miller!"

He pulled into himself and his face turned white. "I won't." But he had his fingers crossed behind his back because he was going to go back and play with Honey and eat rolls and talk to Kandy any time he pleased. Teddy Jo wasn't his boss even if she thought she was. He was seven years old and not a baby. She sure had to stop treating him like one.

"Did you hear her say she wanted someone dead?" asked Teddy Jo in a strained voice.

"You made that up!" cried Paul, stopping short. "She's nice and I know she is!"

Teddy Jo glared down at him and finally he

dropped his eyes to the cracked sidewalk and watched little black ants making a hill with bits of sand.

She rushed down the sidewalk. She had to call Grandpa and tell him what Cathy had said and what she'd overheard Mrs. Sloan say. He would know what to do. He would protect them and keep them safe. He'd be able to convince Paul to stay away from there even though they had a dog. She heard Paul's little feet slapping on the sidewalk trying to keep up with her, but she didn't slow down. She had to get him home where she could watch him.

Paul puffed at her side and wanted desperately to stop, but he knew he didn't dare or she'd grab him and drag him and then everyone would see. He burned with embarrassment just thinking about it.

At the house Teddy Jo unlocked the front door and opened it and heat rushed out. She quickly opened windows as Paul turned on the TV to a game show. She saw Cathy running toward the Miller house. Teddy Jo opened the door and Cathy rushed in, her face red, her eyes wide.

"What happened?"

Teddy Jo swallowed hard. "Nothing."

"Why did you leave so soon?"

Teddy Jo didn't want to say. "Want to play Monopoly?"

"No. Come to my house and play Space Invaders."

She looked at Paul. "Can he come, too?"

"Jim's not home."

She couldn't leave Paul. He'd take off for the pink house and then what would happen to him? Why wasn't Linda home to take care of Paul? Why couldn't she ever do what she wanted, when she wanted?

Paul felt her eyes on him and he turned and looked at her, then quickly turned back to the TV where a woman was jumping up and down, screaming because she'd won $5000. He'd jump up and down and scream if he won money, too. Then he'd buy a dog.

Teddy Jo pulled Cathy to the kitchen with her and they drank Vernors ginger ale and ate stale potato chips and talked. Teddy Jo made sure they didn't talk about the strangers in the pink house. She wasn't ready to talk about them yet. She forced her mind off them and onto the plans for her birthday party. Finally the excitement about her party filled her and she almost bounced on her chair as she talked. No strangers in a pink house would stop her from being excited about her very first birthday party!

5. A Talk with Mom

Teddy Jo tried to swallow but her mouth was cotton-dry. She tugged nervously at her dirty tee shirt as she walked slowly into the kitchen. Mom stood at the sink just finishing the last of the supper dishes. The kitchen still smelled like pizza and garlic bread.

Carol turned, unsmiling, and studied Teddy Jo. Carol was dressed in yellow shorts that showed off her long, tanned legs, and a yellow suntop that hugged her body. Her dark brown hair curled around her slender face and hung down to her shoulders. "Why do you keep looking at me as if I have a hook nose and buck teeth, Teddy Jo?"

"I didn't. I wasn't." Teddy Jo clutched the back of a kitchen chair. "You're real pretty, Mom."

Carol lifted her chin and patted her hair. "Do you think so?"

Teddy Jo nodded. "I guess you're one of the prettiest moms around."

Carol eyed Teddy Jo suspiciously. "What's this leading up to?"

"Well . . . ."

"What?"

Teddy Jo sank down on the chair and locked her fingers together. "I am going to be eleven next week."

"I remember. I was there when you were born."

"I want to have a birthday party." She saw Mom's hesitation and rushed on. "I'll plan it and do all the work and Cathy said she'd help me. Can I, Mom? Please? Please?"

Carol moistened her pink lips and sighed.

"I'll stop asking for a dog if you'll do this for me."

Carol laughed. "The day you stop asking for a dog will be the day you draw your last breath." She crumpled the towel and dropped it on the counter. "All right, Teddy Jo. But only if you do all the planning and the work. And I don't want it in here where all those little kids will ruin the carpets and furniture."

Teddy Jo jumped up and almost flung herself against Mom, then stopped and flushed hotly. "Thanks, Mom. We'll have it in the yard and we'll do it when you're at work and Grandpa can come over."

"You'll clean up any mess."

"I will." She dived for the bottom cupboard

drawer where she'd stuffed the plans and spread them out on the table. "Here's a list of food I want. If you'll give me the money, I'll go to the store myself."

Carol read the list with a frown. "I'll give you money and you'll have to make it stretch to pay for everything. And you can't beg more from Grandpa. Understand?"

"I won't. I promise. Oh, this is going to be the best birthday I've ever had!"

"You have to let Paul and Linda join in."

Her heart sank, but she only nodded. She wouldn't do anything to stop this party. No way would she let Paul or Linda ruin her party!

Carol pulled out a chair and sat across from Teddy Jo. "I just noticed today that someone moved into the pink house down the street. Do you know who it was?"

Teddy Jo stiffened and the pencil fell from her fingers to the table and rolled to the center. "Paul and I met them in the park this morning."

"Who are they and how many?"

Teddy Jo forced back a shiver. "A girl my age named Kandy Kane." She spelled it the way Kandy had and Mom laughed and shook her head. "And her grandma is Anna Sloan. And Cathy's mom said that there is something strange about them."

"And is there?"

Teddy Jo hesitated. Should she tell Mom? She took a deep breath. "I think so. They invited us in for orange juice." Suddenly her eyes sparkled. "They've got a microwave oven just like you want and Mrs. Sloan made rolls in it and they were delicious."

"And that's strange?" Carol laughed and shook her head.

Teddy Jo's stomach tightened and she picked up the pencil and looked at the chewed eraser intently. "She talked on the phone to someone named Arlo and she said she wanted some guy dead."

Carol laughed lightly. "Oh, Teddy Jo, you're making all that up."

Her eyes flashed. "No, I'm not! I heard it and I got Paul out of there so she couldn't do anything to us. Maybe she wanted us dead, too, and I don't want that to happen even if we would go to heaven to live with Jesus."

"You heard her wrong, Teddy Jo!" Carol snapped. "We don't have murderers in this little town."

Teddy Jo clamped her mouth shut tight. She knew what she'd heard, but she wouldn't argue about it and make Mom so mad that she'd call off the birthday party.

"I don't want you telling that story around. Do you hear me?" Carol leaned toward Teddy Jo. "I mean it! We don't want any trouble from our new neighbors."

"All right, Mom," said Teddy Jo meekly.

Carol gave her a sharp look of surprise, then

44

stood up. "Kandy Kane. Who would name a girl Kandy Kane?"

Teddy Jo wrinkled her small nose. Who would name a girl Theodora Josephine and call her Teddy Jo?

"Will Kandy be in your class at school?"

"She'll be going home before then and Mrs. Sloan will live alone." Then she could have all the dead bodies she wanted without anyone interfering.

"If I had more time I'd walk down the street and get acquainted with them."

"Mom, do you ever wish you didn't have to work?"

Carol lifted her fine brows. "Why do you ask?"

"Don't you ever wish you could stay home like Mrs. Brent does?"

Carol shrugged. "I don't have a choice. I work so we can eat and so you can have clothes to wear."

"If I was big I'd get a job and make a million dollars so you could stay home."

"Why, Teddy Jo, thank you. That's sure nice of you."

She flushed with pleasure and looked down at her scribbled birthday notes. Finally she looked up. "If I could sell my paintings and drawings right now I'll bet I could make enough money so you wouldn't have to work."

Carol laughed and shook her head. "Dream

on, little girl. Who would buy your stuff?"

Teddy Jo sat very still as the hurt cramped her stomach and squeezed her heart until she thought all the blood was drained out.

"You've got to do real work in this life to get anywhere. Art is for the dreamers of this world. You won't be a dreamer, Teddy Jo! You are going to train for a job that'll make you money to live on, money to pay your bills. That's the only way to make it. You can't walk on some cloud and think some great day you'll be an artist. It's OK to play around with drawing and painting. I did when I was your age. But it didn't get me anywhere. Did it? I'm right here and I wouldn't even be here if Dad hadn't helped us out." Carol twirled a piece of hair around her finger and Teddy Jo blinked back hot tears.

"I had dreams once of being a great artist. I had great dreams! Then I got married and had three kids and no money and where did the grand dreams go?"

Teddy Jo wanted to run to her room and bury her head and scream at the top of her lungs, but her legs were too weak to support her. She sagged against the table and Mom's words hit her, blow after blow.

"Dreams are for rich folks. We've got to keep our noses to the grindstone and work and work and work and maybe someday put enough away to retire on and to live on without going to a place for old poor folks."

46

"Grandpa would've helped you," whispered Teddy Jo hoarsely.

Carol laughed bitterly and shook her head. "Your grandpa was different back then. He wouldn't help anybody, not even his own kid. He wanted me to work for what I got. And I worked, but I got nothing."

Teddy Jo trembled. Sounds of the TV drifted from the living room. She wanted to look at Mom, but she couldn't lift her head.

"You think of some training you want to take and you leave all those thoughts of being an artist behind while you're young." Carol flicked the dishtowel. "I've got work to do. When do I have time to sit around and talk for hours? You run along and think about your birthday party."

Teddy Jo clutched the papers and stumbled from the kitchen and leaned weakly against the wall in the hall. Paul's bedroom door was open and she could smell the ammonia smell that meant he'd wet his bed again. She gritted her teeth and narrowed her eyes. Wouldn't he ever learn? She'd asked him just this morning and he'd said that he hadn't wet. But maybe it hadn't been last night. Maybe the smell was in his blanket from all the other times. If she could get her hands on him right now, he'd sure be sorry. But he was with Dad watching TV and she sure couldn't say anything now or Dad would get mad and whip Paul hard.

Slowly she walked to her room and softly

closed her door. She stood there, her thin chest rising and falling, tears filling her blue eyes. She saw her paints and the canvas that Grandpa had stretched for her and the pain welled up and up and she ran to her bed and flung herself down and sobbed brokenly.

6. Grandpa

The doorknob turned and Teddy Jo shot up
and instantly brushed away her tears. Paul
walked in and she leaped up, her fists doubled
at her sides.

"How dare you just walk in, Paul?"

His face turned sickly gray and he backed
toward the door. He swallowed nervously.
"You said we were going to the park," he said
barely above a whisper.

"Oh." She flushed. "I guess I forgot."

"Maybe Mrs. Sloan and Kandy will be there
with Honey."

"Then we aren't going!"

Paul blinked and his heart raced in alarm.
They just had to go! He had to see Honey and
pet her and run with her and pretend she was
his dog. He lifted his head high and dragged
out all his hidden courage. "Then, I'll go by

myself! Grandpa said he'd meet us there and I won't be alone for long. You can stay home if you want."

Teddy Jo gulped and stared in astonishment at Paul. "You sure do think you're big, don't you?"

He turned and ran out before Teddy Jo made him lose all his nerve. He ran to the front door and jerked it open before Dad could look up from watching "The Michigan Sportsman" on TV and tell him to be quiet.

Teddy Jo saw the door close after Paul and she shook her head to clear her surprised brain. Dad glanced at her, then back at the TV. He had his favorite fishing rod in his hand and she knew he was comparing it with the one the man on TV was using.

Slowly Teddy Jo walked to the front door and stepped outside. The late afternoon sun scorched her head and she wished it would cool off soon in case a good soccer game was going on in the park. She sighed heavily. Why even think about a soccer game? She couldn't play well when she was feeling this terrible. Maybe she'd never feel good again. Maybe she'd never speak to Mom again. For sure she'd never, ever talk to Mom about art again!

Mrs. Brent called to her and waved and Teddy Jo waved, but didn't stop. If she talked to Mrs. Brent, she'd burst into tears for sure. Oh, how she wanted to fling herself into Mrs.

Brent's arms to be held close, even to be kissed softly on the cheek.

Tears filled her eyes and she rapidly blinked them away. She was no baby to cry over every little hurt, was she?

Two cars and a silver pickup drove past. A cat mewed at the curb, then ambled across the street. Teddy Jo peeked at the pink house, then quickly away. Should she tell Grandpa about the strangers in the pink house? She frowned and abruptly shook her head. He might get mad like Mom had and tell her she was dumb. But maybe he wouldn't. Oh, but she couldn't take a chance! Her stomach tightened. She loved Grandpa more than anyone else and it would be awful if he got mad at her.

She stopped just inside the park and looked across the soft green grass at all the boys and girls running and shouting. Just then she spotted Paul with Mrs. Sloan and Kandy. Her heart raced and she frantically looked around to see who could help her get Paul away from them if she needed help. Oh, why hadn't Paul listened to her?

Just then Paul turned and saw her and his hands shook as he wrapped his arms around Honey. Teddy Jo sure couldn't make him leave Honey just when he was making friends with her. He looked helplessly up at Mrs. Sloan but he didn't want to tell her that his dumb sister thought Mrs. Sloan could kill someone. Mrs. Sloan might never let him pet Honey again.

Teddy Jo clenched and unclenched her fists. Her skin prickled with sweat and she rubbed her hands over her bare legs. Just then she heard her name spoken and she whirled around to find Grandpa walking toward her. He was dressed in matching tan shirt and pants and he looked as big as the tree near the swings. He smiled and her heart leaped with love. She flung herself into his powerful arms and he lifted her high in a bear hug that almost cracked her ribs. She laughed with joy as she breathed in the smell of him. She rubbed her cheek against his and felt the dark stubble of whiskers.

"How are you, Teddy Jo?"

She hesitated, then smiled and shrugged. "My birthday is next week and I'm going to have a party. Will you come?"

"Sure. Nothing would keep me away from a birthday party for my Teddy Bear Jo." He laughed his booming laugh and she laughed with him.

"I'll be eleven years old."

"Now, that's sure old. You'll have gray hair before you know it."

"Oh, Grandpa!"

He looked past her, then frowned slightly. "Who's Paul with?"

Teddy Jo bit her bottom lip and her heart beat faster. "I guess we'd better go get him. He

52

sure is having fun with that dog."

"It's a pretty little cocker spaniel. But Paul shouldn't be talking to strangers."

Teddy Jo tugged Grandpa's big hand that was hard and strong from years of working. "Paul won't listen to me much. But I'll bet he'll listen to you, Grandpa." She smiled secretly behind her hand. Paul was sure going to be sorry that he hadn't obeyed her.

"Did you finish your painting?" he asked as they walked slowly across the park.

Abruptly she stopped. "I can't finish it," she said in a strangled voice.

He frowned. "Why? You were doing so well with it."

"I'll never be an artist!" Her blue eyes flashed and she lifted her chin defiantly.

He studied her thoughtfully. Laugh lines spread from the corners of his blue eyes to his gray hair. "We'll talk about this later, Teddy Jo. First, I want to get Paul and have a word with that young man."

Teddy Jo walked along beside Grandpa, part of her thankful that he didn't say more about her art and part of her disappointed, too.

Paul jumped up as Grandpa stopped in front of him. "Look at Honey, Grandpa! She loves me!"

Grandpa looked from the dog to the woman and girl. Teddy Jo stood quietly, her hands locked behind her back.

"I'm Anna Sloan and this is my granddaughter, Kandy Kane," said Anna as she held out her hand. Grandpa hesitated, then clasped her hand. "We just moved into the pink house on Oak Street."

He smiled and Teddy Jo wanted to grab him and yank him out of the woman's grasp. "I'm Ed Korman, and Paul and Teddy Jo here are my grandchildren. They live on Oak Street also."

"I know," said Anna. "We met this morning."

Grandpa shot a searching look at Teddy Jo and she dropped her head. "Welcome to Middle Lake," said Grandpa warmly, still holding Anna's hand.

Paul looked smugly at Teddy Jo and she wanted to strangle him, but she stood still as Grandpa and Mrs. Sloan talked. Paul continued to pet Honey and play with her floppy ears.

Kandy studied Ed Korman and wished that her grandpa was still alive and with them right now. She glanced at Teddy Jo and wondered why she was so mad.

"Teddy Jo's having a birthday party next week, the twenty-third," said Grandpa. "We'd like to have you both come if you can."

Teddy Jo caught back a gasp of alarm. She looked helplessly up at Grandpa, but he was busy smiling at Mrs. Sloan and she was busy saying that she and Kandy would love to come.

"Bring Honey with you," said Paul excitedly,

54

his blue eyes sparkling. "We can play together."

"Is it all right if we bring her?" asked Mrs. Sloan.

"Of course," said Grandpa before Teddy Jo could open her mouth.

Teddy Jo's heart sank. What if Mrs. Sloan brought poison to sprinkle in the Kool-Aid? She just might decide that she wanted all the kids on Oak Street dead. Teddy Jo shivered and stepped closer to Grandpa.

7. A Walk to Grandpa's Place

Teddy Jo screwed up her face and thought hard as she walked beside Paul along the dirt road that led to Grandpa's place. "If I could have any dog in the whole world I'd pick a black dog." She screwed her face up harder and thought harder. Paul was getting even better at this game than she was. She'd have to make it really good. "I'd pick a black, fuzzy dog about up to here." She measured to her knee. "And he'd have curly hair and a black button nose and hair over his eyes and he'd come only when I called him."

Paul nodded hard. He loved this game more than any other they played. He was bursting to tell his part, but he knew he had to wait until Teddy Jo was absolutely done or she'd call herself the winner.

"He'd know all kinds of tricks, but he wouldn't do them unless I told him to."

"Is that all?"

Teddy Jo rubbed her hands down her shorts
and wrinkled her forehead. A grasshopper
landed on her sandaled foot. She shook her foot
and it hopped off without spitting any tobacco
juice on her. "I'm still thinking." She couldn't
think of anything right offhand, but she didn't
want Paul to jump right in and start talking.
She stopped for a minute and beamed with
excitement. "He'd sleep right at the foot of my
bed every night and he'd wake me up if a fire
started in the house or a burglar broke in." She
swaggered along beside Paul, finally finished.
He sure couldn't top that. "OK, Paul. Your
turn."

Paul kicked a rock into the weed-covered
ditch. He sure wished he'd thought of that. It
would be great to have a dog sleep on his bed.
He looked up and his blue eyes sparkled. "My
dog would sleep at the foot of my bed and he'd
wake me up two times in the night so I could
go to the bathroom!" Now, that was sure to get
him the winning point, but Teddy Jo only
shrugged and he knew he'd have to do better.

He scratched his head right where the hot
sun was making it itch. "I want a dog that is
small and golden with long floppy ears."

"That's Honey and she's already taken."

"Well, I can sure have one just like her!"

"Is that all?"

"No. I've got more." He pulled his dirty tee
shirt down over his baggy shorts. He took time

58

out to tie his tennis shoe and he searched his brain for something truly great, something that would make Teddy Jo admit it was great. Finally he thought of something and he jumped up and ran to catch up to Teddy Jo. She looked down at him with a frown and he knew she was thinking that he didn't really have anything more to say. He'd sure fool her!

"I'd have a golden dog that came only when *I* called her."

"I already said that."

"And she'd do tricks, even more tricks than your dog."

"Not so!"

He suddenly wished he had pockets. He'd stick his hands in his pockets and walk along just like the big fourth-graders he knew that thought they were so great. "My dog would be a girl dog and she'd have five puppies and I'd get to keep them all!" Nobody could beat that, not even Teddy Jo!

She stopped dead and looked down at Paul in awe. That was the best yet and he'd thought of it. Maybe he wasn't as dumb as she thought he was. "I sure wish I'd thought of that."

He glowed and thrust out his thin chest, and he felt as if he'd just been awarded the Nobel Peace Prize. He'd heard about that on the news last night and it was the greatest prize he could think of at the time.

"You did great, Paul." He really had, so it didn't bother her to admit it to him.

He grinned from ear to ear. It wasn't often that Teddy Jo gave him a compliment. The trouble was, he couldn't come up with anything better for next time. For a minute he was sad, then he thought of the golden dog and her five puppies playing on his bed and he pictured himself plopped down in the middle of them and he laughed right out loud.

Teddy Jo heard it and she knew he was in a good mood and she decided this was a good time to bring up the birthday party. "Paul, I want you to stay in the house when I have my party."

He stopped a minute in surprise, then continued walking beside her. A truck drove past, almost choking him with dust. "Why?"

"It's my party and I want my friends there and not a seven-year-old kid brother." She saw him pull into himself and she felt bad. "You can take Honey and Grandpa and Mrs. Sloan in the living room and talk to them and play with Honey."

"She can't go into the house. Mom said no dogs allowed in the house." He felt hot tears at the backs of his eyes and it made him mad. How could he be such a baby to cry over a dumb birthday party?

"Then you can go around to the side of the house where I won't be, and play with Honey there."

He shrugged, but couldn't speak without her knowing he was ready to cry.

60

"I sure wish Grandpa hadn't invited Mrs. Sloan and Kandy Kane. Kandy Kane. Ha! If I had a name like that I'd sure be mad."

"I like it."

"You'd like anything."

He hunched his shoulders and looked like a baby bird sitting down in a nest with its head pulled down and its wings up. He was glad when they finally ran up Grandpa's short drive.

They heard a sander humming and Teddy Jo ran to the garage and peeked in where Grandpa had his workshop. He looked up, smiled happily, and turned off the sander. He brushed sawdust off himself, then walked to the door and ruffled Paul's hair and squeezed Teddy Jo's shoulder.

"You kids hot and thirsty after that walk? Want orange juice? Kool-Aid? Water?"

Paul nodded at each thing. Teddy Jo said she wanted orange juice from Florida. She caught hold of one of Grandpa's big hands and Paul the other and they walked around to the back door and into the cool kitchen.

After they finished drinking Grandpa said, "I've got a big surprise out in the pen."

Paul jumped to his feet, wiping his hand across his mouth. "What?"

Teddy Jo rushed to the door. She couldn't wait to see what kind of animal Grandpa was taking care of this time.

"Don't go into the pen," Grandpa called after her.

She ran across the grassy yard, then stopped short. Paul puffed up beside her and looked through the wire fence.

"A dog!" cried Teddy Jo.

"No." Grandpa laughed softly. "It's a fox, a young fox."

"A fox," whispered Paul. He wriggled all over inside just thinking about how cute and cuddly the fox was. He wanted to slip through the gate and pick up the red fox and hold it tight.

"It's not tame at all," said Grandpa. "See its paw, the right front one? It was caught in a trap and I found it and set it free. It'll be just fine in a couple of weeks."

"He's so cute," said Teddy Jo. It was as cute as any puppy she'd ever seen and it was hard to stand outside the pen and just look at it. She wanted to hold it and stroke it and whisper to it. But she knew it was wild and that she couldn't.

Finally Paul ran off to play on the tire swing and Grandpa slipped his arm around Teddy Jo.

"We have some talking to do," he said softly.

Her stomach tightened. She'd hoped that he'd forgotten about what she'd said about never being an artist. But Grandpa never forgot anything. She licked her dry lips and looked down at a bug crawling in the grass.

Grandpa walked her to a faded red bench and sat down with her. "Now, tell me what happened to change your mind about art?"

She swallowed hard. "Do I have to?"

"Not at all, but I can help you if you talk to me." He took one of her hands between his work-roughened hands. "You are an artist, Teddy Bear Jo. God has given you a great talent. We aren't going to let anything stop you from putting your talent to use."

She slid closer to Grandpa so that she was touching him. "Mom said I shouldn't dream such big dreams. She said I won't make it as an artist and that I might as well know it now."

Grandpa gathered her close. "I'm so sorry! Your mom is wonderful and I love her, but she sees things different than we do. I hurt her badly when she was young. I wasn't a good dad to her and she can't forget it. But, Teddy Jo, I'm different now. You're different. We are Christians and we have new spirits. Your mom doesn't. But she will as soon as she's born again."

Teddy Jo sniffed and nodded.

"Don't let her words hurt you. Don't be mad at her. She doesn't know what she does to you when she says you won't make it as an artist. She thinks she's helping you. You must forgive her, Teddy Jo. Push out the anger and bitterness that you feel toward her, and you go on with your art."

She thought of the terrible words and the pain and she didn't think she could just forget it. "She hates me, Grandpa."

He kissed the top of her head. "She doesn't

hate you. She hasn't learned how to love yet, but she will. Give her time. You keep right on loving her with God's help."

Teddy Jo sighed. If Grandpa said so, she'd do it. "I will, Grandpa. And I will forgive her. But I guess I'd better not show her my artwork."

"One of these days she'll ask to see it and then you can take her to your room and show her everything you've painted or drawn."

She thought of what a grand day that would be and she smiled. She scooted around, then flung her arms around Grandpa's neck and kissed his leathery cheek.

8. Carol

Teddy Jo pushed the key into the front door lock, then lifted her head and listened with a frown. The TV was playing. Had Paul left it on when they went to the park this morning? Teddy Jo pressed her lips tightly together. He'd sure be in trouble if he had! She'd make sure he remembered to turn it off next time.

Quickly she turned the key and pushed the door open, then stared in surprise at the top of the head sticking over the back of the couch. Mom was home!

Teddy Jo dropped the key back in the planter and rushed to Carol's side. "Mom! Why are you home? Are you sick?"

Carol frowned and tucked the bright afghan tighter around her even though the room was warm. "Don't make so much noise, Teddy Jo. My head is splitting. I had to leave work early. Where's Paul? And Linda?"

Teddy Jo kicked Paul's dirty sock out of sight under the couch. "Paul's over playing with Jimmy Norton and Linda went home with one of her friends. They'll both be back in an hour." She sat on the edge of a chair and wrapped her arms around her knees. She sure was glad that she and Grandpa had had that talk yesterday or she wouldn't have been able to sit here with Mom. "It was funny to have you home when I walked in. I couldn't figure out who had the TV on."

Carol leaned her head back and closed her eyes and Teddy Jo immediately jumped up.

"Are you all right? Do you want a cup of tea? Shall I make you a sandwich?"

Carol's eyes snapped open and she stared at Teddy Jo as if she'd never seen her before. "What has happened to you, Theodora Josephine?"

Teddy Jo twisted her toe in the carpet. "What do you mean?"

"You're so nice. What did you do wrong? Are you keeping a secret from me?"

Teddy Jo grinned and hunched her shoulders. "I told you it's because I'm a Christian. I'm learning to be like Jesus and like Grandpa. It sure is funny to be nice instead of bad all the time."

Carol smiled stiffly. "Yes, well, I thought you'd be over that by now. Keep it up if you can. I think Grandpa deserves a reward for helping you to change."

"Me, too."

"If you want to make a cup of tea for me, then go ahead. That would be nice. Just don't spill anything or burn yourself."

"I won't!" Teddy Jo ran to the kitchen, her heart jumping happily. She was going to do something nice for Mom. No way would she mess up now!

The water finally boiled and Teddy Jo carefully filled Mom's favorite flowered cup with water. She dipped in the tea bag and watched the water turn light brown, then darker. She pulled out the bag and carried it across the counter to the little tray that Mom used especially for her tea bag.

Just then Carol walked in and sat at the table. "I'll have my tea here. How about a piece of toast to go with it?"

"Sure, and I won't burn it either." Teddy Jo walked slowly to the table, balancing the cup of tea. Not one drop spilled. She stepped back with a wide smile, then turned and pulled the bread out of the bread drawer.

As it toasted she turned to Mom. Carol smiled and Teddy Jo smiled. The toast popped up and Teddy Jo buttered it and carried it to Mom.

The back doorbell rang and Teddy Jo jumped, then ran to the door. She peeked out the glass, then frowned. Mrs. Sloan stood just outside as if she belonged there.

"Who is it?" asked Carol sharply.

"Mrs. Sloan."

"Well, let her in, for heaven's sake."

Teddy Jo slowly opened the door. Honey wasn't with Mrs. Sloan and neither was Kandy.

"I came by to see if I could help you get ready for your birthday party, Teddy Jo." She walked in and Teddy Jo swallowed hard, her hands suddenly icy cold.

"Hello, Mrs. Sloan. I'm Carol Miller, Teddy Jo's mother."

Mrs. Sloan walked forward with her hand out. "I'm glad to meet you. I walked Kandy over to Cathy's house, so I thought I'd stop in and help Teddy Jo. We're excited about coming to her birthday party on Thursday."

Carol smiled tensely. "Yes, well, I wish I could be here, but I have to work. I'm home today only because I don't feel well."

"Is there anything I can do?"

"I'm taking care of Mom," cut in Teddy Jo.

"Fix Mrs. Sloan a cup of tea, Teddy Jo."

"Call me Anna." She sat down as if she belonged.

Teddy Jo made a cup of tea and carried it to the table. Her hand shook so much she slopped the tea on the floor and almost on Mrs. Sloan. "Sorry." Her face burned and she quickly wiped up the spill.

Anna Sloan and Carol talked quietly at the table, and Teddy Jo stood at the sink wondering if she should stay or leave. Just as she

68

decided that she'd leave, the back door opened and Grandpa stepped in. She squealed and flung herself against him, and his arms wrapped around her and held her close. He smelled like outdoors and peppermint and wood shavings. He was dressed in matching dark green pants and shirt that he'd bought from Sears in Grand Rapids.

"How's my Teddy Jo today?" His blue eyes crinkled at the corners as he smiled. His gray hair was mussed from the wind outdoors.

"I'm just fine, Grandpa, but Mom came home early from work with a bad headache."

Grandpa looked over Teddy Jo's head, then walked to the table. "Hello, Carol. Anna. It's a pleasure to see you again." Grandpa looked at Anna for a long moment. Then he finally pulled his eyes away from her and turned back to Carol. "I'm sorry that you don't feel well. Is there anything that I can do?"

"Not a thing."

"Maybe fix supper." He pulled Teddy Jo close to his side. "Teddy Jo and I can make a good meal for the family."

"That would be nice," said Carol weakly.

"And I'll help," said Anna Sloan, smiling. "I'd enjoy that."

"Me, too," said Grandpa and Teddy Jo didn't like the soft look he gave Mrs. Sloan.

"Why don't you stay and eat with us, Anna?" asked Carol with a smile. "Teddy Jo can run

and tell Kandy to come here when she's done
playing with Cathy."

"Stay, Anna," said Grandpa. "I'd like that."

"I'd be glad to, Ed."

Carol stood up. "If you'll excuse me, I'll go
rest awhile before supper. My headache should
be gone by then." She walked to the door, then
turned. "The tea was good, Teddy Jo."

"Thanks." Teddy Jo stood taller and smiled.
"I'll help make supper, too, and it'll be good."
Besides, she had to make sure Anna Sloan
didn't do anything bad to the food.

Grandpa pulled out a chair and sat facing
Anna Sloan. Teddy Jo hesitated, then sat close
to Grandpa. She sure wouldn't give Mrs. Sloan
a chance to hurt Grandpa.

"I'm thankful that I found such a nice town
to live in," said Anna. She curled her hand
around her cup. "I like a small town."

"It is nice here," said Grandpa. "And close
enough to the city to give folks jobs. Carol and
Larry work at Turno Industries in Grand
Rapids on the day shift."

"I've driven past there, I think. It's just off
28th Street near Division, isn't it?"

Grandpa nodded and they continued to talk
while Teddy Jo squirmed impatiently. How
could Grandpa enjoy talking to Mrs. Sloan?
Why didn't he just send her home so he could
cook supper?

"Teddy Jo, run and tell Kandy to come here
when she's ready to leave Cathy's," said

70

Grandpa. "Anna and I will start supper in a few minutes."

Teddy Jo hesitated. Should she leave Grandpa alone with Mrs. Sloan? "I could call Cathy."

"You don't want to stay here and listen to us," said Grandpa. "Run along and have fun with your friends." He gave her a little push and she flushed and ran to the door and out into the bright sunlight. Oh, why had they ever met Mrs. Sloan and Kandy and Honey?

Slowly Teddy Jo walked to Cathy's backyard where the girls were jumping on the giant black inner tube that Cathy's uncle had given her from his big machine.

"Hi," said Teddy Jo.

Cathy stopped and ran to her. "Kandy came to play. She's nice. I don't think there's anything wrong with her grandma."

Teddy Jo wanted to disagree, but Kandy ran to her and she couldn't talk about it. "You and your grandma are having supper with us tonight," Teddy Jo said instead.

Kandy jumped up and down, shouting excitedly. "Shall I go home with you now?"

"We don't have to go yet."

"I have to go to gymnastics practice now," said Cathy. "But you can stay and bounce on my inner tube." She said good-bye and ran to the house.

Kandy smiled hesitantly. "What do you want to do?"

"I don't care."

71

They walked to the inner tube and sat on it and looked at each other.

"Did my grandma tell you her secret?"

"What secret?" Teddy Jo's stomach fluttered nervously.

"I guess she didn't, so I can't." Kandy frowned. Grandma had said that soon she'd be able to tell her new friends the secret. Kandy peeked at Teddy Jo from under her lashes. What would Teddy Jo say if she knew that Anna Sloan was a murder mystery writer, a very famous one? Kandy wanted to tell everyone, but Grandma had said it was a secret and that she wrote under the name of Nelson Grandby so that she wouldn't lose her privacy.

"I hate secrets!" Teddy Jo was aching to know Mrs. Sloan's secret and she wanted to pry it out of Kandy, but she just sat quietly.

"Some secrets are fun," said Kandy. Was Teddy Jo mad at her because she wouldn't tell?

Teddy Jo kicked the grass. Mrs. Sloan was probably a secret killer. No wonder she didn't want anyone to know. Suddenly Teddy Jo jumped up. "Let's go to my house." She had to protect Grandpa any way she could.

"Shall we play house?"

"We'll see." First she wanted to make sure Grandpa was still alive. She burst through the back door, then stopped short. Grandpa and Mrs. Sloan stood near the sink, laughing together. Teddy Jo turned to Kandy. "Let's go

to my room to play." She had to get away
before she got mad at Grandpa for liking Mrs.
Sloan. She ran to her bedroom with Kandy
beside her.

9. The Birthday Party

Teddy Jo blew up a red balloon until it was as big as the yellow and green ones, then she tied it and put it on a stick. She stood back and looked at the bouquet of balloons. It sure looked beautiful. Everything did. She rubbed her hand across the paper tablecloth on the picnic table. It was white with wide borders of colored balloons. There wasn't a wind, so everything on the table sat just as she'd placed it with Cathy's help.

"Happy birthday, Teddy Jo," said Jane Brent.

Teddy Jo looked up and smiled, then gasped in surprise. Mrs. Brent carried a large two-layer birthday cake decorated with flowers and bows and eleven candles. On top was written, "Happy Birthday, Teddy Jo."

Jane set it in the middle of the table, then stood back with a pleased smile. She was

dressed in tan slacks and a white blouse. "I
know you have another cake, but I wanted to
make a special one for you because I love you."
She tipped up Teddy Jo's face and kissed her
on each cheek. "Happy, happy birthday. God's
very special blessings on you now and forever."

Teddy Jo blinked back tears and smiled until
she thought her face would crack. "That's the
best cake I ever saw. Thank you."

Mike ran into the yard, carrying a large
package. His camera hung from his wrist.
"Happy birthday, Teddy Jo. Mom wants to
take a picture of you with your cake before we
cut it." Mike set the gift on the gift table that
Cathy had decorated, then handed the camera
to his mother.

Teddy Jo hooked her tangled hair behind her
ears and stood proudly beside the decorated
table.

"Hold it!" Jane aimed the camera, then
clicked. She pushed the film forward, then
aimed again and clicked again. "Mike, stand
with Teddy Jo. Pretend you're presenting her
with her present."

"Aw, Mom."

Jane laughed. "Just do it, Mike."

"You don't have to," said Teddy Jo.

"That's all right." Mike picked up the
package and held it out to Teddy Jo. She
reached for it. Her hands itched to grab it and
rip off the bright paper and see what was
inside. "It's not just from me alone. Some of us

76

went together to buy it for you. I hope you don't care."

"I don't." She'd never received presents from anyone but her own family, so anything seemed fantastic.

"That's enough for now. I'll take more pictures later when the guests come." Jane put the camera near a bag of potato chips. "Here come Anna Sloan and Kandy."

Paul rushed out the back door where he'd been waiting for sight of Honey. "Hi, Mrs. Sloan."

"Hello, Paul."

Paul dropped on his knees and hugged Honey tightly. "I wish I had a dog just like you."

"Happy birthday, Teddy Jo," said Anna and Kandy together, then laughed.

"Grandpa's not here yet," said Teddy Jo.

"He will be, don't worry." Anna smiled. "I spoke on the phone with him last night. I wanted to tell him how much I enjoyed having dinner with all of you the other day."

"It was fun," said Kandy. "Is your mom here?"

"She's at work. Linda's here." Teddy Jo motioned for Linda to join them and Linda slowly walked from the corner of the house to the others. She liked the looks of the cake and tables and she wished she could have a birthday party. How in the world did Teddy Jo get enough friends to have a party? And why wasn't she dressed better? Didn't she know she had a hole in her tee shirt? Somebody should make her go back inside and brush her hair and wash her face. Wouldn't she ever, ever grow up?

"How are you, Linda?" asked Jane Brent with a smile. "You look very pretty today. I think I'll take a picture of you, too."

Linda smiled. She liked having her picture taken. Some day maybe she'd be a model. She'd make lots of money and buy a big house that would be just hers and everyone would know her when she walked down the street.

As Jane snapped the picture, Linda saw Grandpa walk around the house. She started toward him, her heart leaping with love, then stopped as Teddy Jo flung herself into his arms. Teddy Jo thought she owned Grandpa just because she'd stayed with him so long last summer.

Slowly Linda walked toward Grandpa and Teddy Jo and she heard him say, "Happy birthday, Teddy Bear Jo. I hope this year's the best year you've ever had!"

Teddy Jo hugged him tighter, then had to greet Cathy and Dara and two other girls who were all arriving together.

Grandpa smiled at Linda. "How are you, Linda?"

She shrugged.

He held out his arms to her and she hesitated, then walked into his arms. It felt so good

78

to have him hug her and tell her that he loved her. She hugged him harder than usual and she didn't want to let him go.

"I'm glad you stayed home today, Linda. I don't get to see much of you. Why don't you come home with me today after the party? You can see the little fox I have, and we can talk."

"Just me?"

He nodded and kissed her cheek, which was pink with the blusher she used. "Just you."

"I'd like that." She had to turn away before she burst into tears. Sometimes she felt very lonely and unloved. But Grandpa really cared. She knew it. She could feel it and she wanted to hang onto that always.

Teddy Jo stood near the gift table and her blue eyes sparkled with excitement. Did she really get to keep the gifts? She wanted to open them now and not wait until after they played games, but Cathy was already calling for everyone to line up. Cathy sure knew how to organize a party.

Teddy Jo saw Paul near the house with Honey and she felt so good about the party and all her friends that she called, "Come and play, Paul. You can stand by me."

Paul gasped, then slowly stood up. He couldn't believe Teddy Jo had actually asked him to join in the games after she'd told him to stay out of sight. He looked uncertainly toward Grandpa and he waved him on. Paul smiled and ran to stand beside Teddy Jo. This was going to be a pretty good party, after all. It might be hard to stand and watch her open all the gifts and know none of them were for him, but at least he could play the games and eat the food, even the fancy cake with her name on it.

Finally the games were over and Teddy Jo stood flushed and excited beside the gift table. She glanced at Grandpa and Mrs. Sloan, then looked quickly away. Today she wouldn't worry about them. Jane Brent snapped another picture and Teddy Jo squared her shoulders and lifted her head higher.

"Open this first," said Mike, pushing the big box toward her.

Shivers of excitement ran up and down her spine as she picked up the box. What could be inside? Carefully she opened the card. It was signed by Grandpa, the Brents, Mrs. Sloan, Kandy, and Floyd Vandecar.

With trembling fingers Teddy Jo tore off the paper and looked at the box and her eyes widened. On the side of the box was a picture of a white and red soccer ball. She looked at Grandpa and he smiled. In a rush she lifted the lid and sure enough it was a soccer ball. A soccer ball of her very own! She wouldn't have to wait for Mike or Marsha to get up a game before she could play. *She* could get up the games and others would come to her to play.

"Thank you," she said with a catch in her voice. It was better than any present she'd ever received.

"Open this one!" cried Dara, pushing a small package toward Teddy Jo. Dara's light blonde hair bobbed as she bounced up and down.

Quickly Teddy Jo tore into the package. She lifted out several barrettes, pieces of colored yarn, ribbons, and several fancy ponytail bands. "Thank you, Dara! Thank you!" She couldn't wait to clip in two of the barrettes to see how they'd look in her dark hair.

She opened the gift from Cathy and blinked back tears when she saw artist's pencils, two paint brushes, and a pad of sketch paper.

Everyone talked and laughed and seemed to be having fun as she finished opening her gifts. She looked around with tears sparkling in her eyes. "Thank you, thank you. Now, let's eat!"

Jane Brent lit the candles and everyone sang "Happy Birthday." Teddy Jo made a wish that Mom and Dad could have come to her party, then she blew out all eleven candles in one big breath.

Mrs. Sloan cut the ice cream and served it while Grandpa filled the paper cups with red punch. Paul took a handful of M & M's and ate them one at a time while he stood in line for the rest of the food. Honey flopped at his feet and rested her head right on his left foot. He didn't want to move.

Teddy Jo looked around at all her friends, then up at Grandpa. "This is the best birthday I've ever had," she whispered.

He bent down and kissed her. "You are

eleven years old now, Teddy Jo. You're growing up."

She leaned her head against his arm, then carried her plate of food to a shaded spot on the lawn and sat cross-legged with her plate balanced on one leg. As long as she lived, she'd remember this birthday party.

She pulled an icing flower off the birthday cake and popped it into her mouth.

10. The Kiss

Teddy Jo slowly pushed back and forth on the tire swing. She saw Paul standing at the fence watching the fox. The others were inside, probably still sitting around the Sunday dinner that Anna Sloan had helped Grandpa fix. She sure was being friendly. And she hadn't killed anyone yet. Since the birthday party two weeks ago she'd spent a lot of time with Grandpa.

Abruptly Teddy Jo jumped off the tire swing and ran to where Linda and Kandy were walking among the black walnut trees. She had to do something to keep from thinking about Grandpa and Mrs. Sloan.

"It's too hot to run," said Linda, fanning herself with her hand.

"I'm not that hot," said Teddy Jo. Her hair hung in two ponytails, one over each ear and she was dressed in a yellow terrycloth sunsuit that Mom and Dad had given her for her birthday.

Kandy flipped her red head. "If I was home right now, I'd be swimming in Lake Huron. The cool water would feel so good!"

"Why doesn't your grandmother go with you and live near you?" asked Teddy Jo hopefully.

"I want her to, but she says she likes it here. She says it's quiet for her work."

"What work?" asked Linda.

Kandy flushed. Grandma had said not to tell yet that she was a murder mystery writer. Kandy shrugged. "Just work. You know, like all grown-ups do."

"Oh." Linda leaned against a tree and looked toward the dirt road. Why didn't a cute boy ride past, see her, and stop to talk to her? Being with Kandy and Teddy Jo was boring. They didn't like to talk about boys.

"I don't think your grandma will really like living in Middle Lake once you're gone," said Teddy Jo. "I bet she'll sell the pink house and move to Port Huron with you."

Kandy shook her head. "No, she won't."

Teddy Jo's heart sank and she knew some- how she'd have to keep Grandpa and Mrs. Sloan apart. "Then I'll bet she'll find so many friends here that she will forget all about Grandpa."

Kandy leaned close to Teddy Jo. "I think she likes your grandpa. I think she *loves* him."

Teddy Jo gasped and Linda laughed in delight.

"And I think Grandpa *loves* her," said Linda with a giggle.

"Grandpa loves everybody!" Teddy Jo doubled her fists and her blue eyes shot off sparks. "Why are we even talking about love? It's a dumb thing to talk about."

"Only to you," snapped Linda. She flipped back her hair and walked away to join Paul near the fox.

"Are you mad, Teddy Jo?"

"Me? Naw."

"What d'you want to do?"

Teddy Jo sighed. "I wish we could go swimming."

"Me, too."

"I'll go ask Grandpa if he'll take us to Sugarbush. I would dive off the dock right into the lake." She could already feel the cool water closing over her head.

"I'd swim to the raft and back and just let the water cool me off." Kandy stroked as if she were swimming, then blew out, turning her head from side to side.

Teddy Jo rolled her eyes and shook her head, then ran toward the house. Mrs. Sloan could stay here with Mom and Dad while Grandpa took them swimming.

She reached the back door several feet ahead of Kandy, and jerked open the screen door. Then she stopped dead, her eyes almost popping out of her head. Grandpa had his arms around Mrs. Sloan and she had her arms around him and they were kissing. Kissing! Just the way Mom and Dad did.

Weakly she closed the screen, then turned and bumped into Kandy. "Get out of my way!" she whispered hoarsely.

Kandy staggered back, her light brown eyes wide with surprise. "Did you ask about swimming?"

Teddy Jo ran toward the trees, tears blurring her vision. Why was Grandpa kissing Mrs. Sloan? Were they in love? Did that mean they might get married? If so, Grandpa would never have time for her!

She scrambled up the large oak to the wide branch where she always sat when she wanted to be alone. She shivered. The rough bark scratched her bare legs.

She heard a rustling and she frowned. Kandy's bright head popped through the leaves and she looked at Teddy Jo in concern.

"What's wrong? Why did you run away?" Kandy steadied herself, then slowly straddled a branch. "Are you sick? Your face sure is white."

"Just leave me alone!" She pressed her chin to her chest and poked out her bottom lip. She felt like Paul, but right now she didn't care. It was awful for Grandpa and Mrs. Sloan to be kissing.

"Are you mad at me?" Kandy frowned. She

sure hadn't done anything to make Teddy Jo mad. Maybe it wasn't even worth it to be friends with her.

"Why did you and your grandma even come here?"

"Your grandpa invited us for dinner."

Teddy Jo's head snapped up. "Not here! I mean here in Middle Lake. You could have moved to another small town where we wouldn't have met you."

"Hey! Do you think you can talk to me like that? I've got feelings, you know. I didn't ask to get to know you and your family. It just happened. So, if you don't like it, that's just too bad for you!" Kandy scrambled down the oak and dropped to the ground. She sure wouldn't hang around such a terrible girl. She'd go get Grandma and tell her she wanted to go home right now.

Teddy Jo peeked down through the branches. All she could see of Kandy was her bright red head as she ran toward the house. She really shouldn't have taken her anger out on Kandy. It wasn't her fault that her grandma couldn't keep her lips to herself.

Teddy Jo leaned back with a dark scowl. Nothing would ever be the same with her and Grandpa. He might even forget about her! She whimpered and shook her head. How could she live if Grandpa forgot her? What would she do if he never again called her Teddy Bear Jo?

No way would she cry!

She'd find a way to make Grandpa forget about Mrs. Sloan.

A slow smile crossed her face and she nodded. She'd tell Grandpa about Mrs. Sloan, that she wanted someone dead. And then Grandpa would tell Mrs. Sloan that he didn't want to be friends, that he never wanted to see her again.

With a low chuckle Teddy Jo scrambled down the tree and dropped to the ground with a thud.

"Teddy Jo," called Linda impatiently. "We're going home now. Will you come on?"

She ran toward the house where everyone was standing to say good-bye. She didn't want to see or speak to Mrs. Sloan, but she couldn't just run to the car or Grandpa would call her back.

Her stomach fluttered as she stopped beside Paul. She listened as everyone talked.

Finally Mrs. Sloan turned to her and smiled and said, "Good-bye, Teddy Jo. I'll see you soon, probably at the park tomorrow."

Teddy Jo bit the inside of her bottom lip, then finally said, "Good-bye." No way would she say she'd see her tomorrow or any other day.

"Get into the car, kids," said Larry, waving toward the car.

Teddy Jo looked at Grandpa and wanted to say good-bye, but he was walking Mrs. Sloan to her car and he had his hand at her waist as they walked.

Paul hugged Honey one last time, then let her go to run after Kandy. "See you in the park," he called. He looked quickly at his family, then ducked his head and walked to the car.

Teddy Jo pushed through to the back seat and sat huddled in the corner. As they backed out she didn't even wave at Grandpa.

"Good-bye!" he called.

She peeked out the window and he saw her and threw her a kiss. She ducked. Let his kiss hit the seat between her and Paul and see if she cared. She sure didn't. Not a bit.

11. A Terrible Mistake

"All right, Teddy Jo. Are you going to tell me what's wrong?" Grandpa folded his arms and leaned against the sink.

Teddy Jo backed up until she bumped into the table. She looked at the dirty dishes that Linda hadn't washed yet, then she looked up at Grandpa. Her mouth felt bone-dry. "Something is strange about Mrs. Sloan. Cathy said her mom said so and I heard Mrs. Sloan talking on the phone and I know she's not the kind of person you'd want to be friends with."

Grandpa stood straight, his large hands at his sides. "What *are* you talking about?"

She swallowed hard. If she continued, maybe he'd get so mad that he'd never want to see her again. Before she lost all her courage she told him about the phone call. "I think she is a murderer."

"Anna is a fine woman. You misunderstood

the phone call." His voice was icy and she shivered.

"I heard right! I'll bet she's just waiting to kill all of us!"

"That's a terrible thing to say."

"But it's true!" Teddy Jo wanted to stamp her foot and yell so that he'd believe her, but she knew Grandpa wouldn't tolerate that.

Grandpa shook his head. "I don't want you to repeat this story to anyone. You'll only cause trouble and pain." He gripped her arms. "Are you making this story up because you don't like Anna?"

"I did not make it up!" She jerked away from Grandpa. "It's true! And I'll tell anyone I want to tell and if enough people know what she's really like, they'll run her out of town."

"No. No, Teddy Jo. You will not do such a terrible thing." His voice was low and stern and his blue eyes were cold with anger. "I'm leaving now so that I don't say or do something that I'll regret. You're a little girl and I must take that into consideration."

He turned toward the kitchen door and she caught his arm. "But it's not time for you to go. You said we'd play a game of Monopoly after supper. You said you'd have supper with us."

"Not now. I'll talk with you when my temper has cooled down." He pulled free and walked out and she stamped her foot and screamed at the top of her lungs.

Suddenly Mom was there and she grabbed

her and shook her and Teddy Jo stopped
screaming and glared at Mom.

"I thought that kind of behavior was all in
the past," said Carol sharply. "What on earth
made you carry on so?"

Teddy Jo jerked away and narrowed her
eyes. "Why should you care? You hate me. You
never listen to me."

"What?" Carol helplessly shook her head.

"I wish Mrs. Brent was my mother!" Teddy
Jo clamped her hands to her hips. "*She* loves
me! She listens to me and she takes me places
and *she* was at my birthday party. She doesn't
go to work and leave her kids alone everyday."

"Why are you doing this, Teddy Jo?" asked
Carol in a strangled voice. "I thought we were
getting along just fine."

"Well, we're not!"

"But you have been so good! You haven't hit
me in a long, long time. You don't throw fits
any longer."

Teddy Jo opened her mouth and screamed
loud and long.

Carol turned and ran down the hall.

"Shut up, Teddy Jo!" shouted Larry. "You
stop that screaming right now and you go tell
your mother that you're sorry. She ran to her
room in tears because of you."

Teddy Jo crossed her arms across her thin
chest and looked down at the floor.

"I was just getting to think you were through
making trouble in this family, but I was wrong.

You won't ever change. You're still the same terrible girl."

The words hammered through the anger. She clamped her hands against the sides of her head.

"You go tell your mother that you're sorry and you do it now!" Larry pointed dramatically down the hallway. Teddy Jo took one look at his angry face and she ran.

She stopped suddenly, then rushed into her room and slammed the door. She just could not talk with Mom yet. She sank to the edge of her bed and picked up the big rag doll that Dara Cook had given her. She rubbed her chin on the doll's yellow yarn hair and picked at the yellow gingham dress.

"Randi, I feel so bad," she whispered against the doll's head. "I shouldn't have screamed and said those terrible things to Mom. But Randi, they are true. She doesn't love me. If I had a little girl I'd love her a whole lot and I'd tell her so. I'd love her and pray for her the way Grandpa does for me and the others in our family."

She stopped and groaned. Grandpa was mad at her and she needed him right now. But he wasn't here and he might not ever want to see her again.

"I'm so alone, Randi," she whispered brokenly. Then she remembered that God was with her, was always with her. He was her heavenly Father and his Spirit lived inside of her.

She closed her eyes. "Heavenly Father, I am so sorry for getting mad at Mom and for saying bad things to her. I need you to help me right now. I will be nice because you want me to be nice. Please help me to be nice. And help me to make Mom feel better. I love you and I do love my family. I guess I love Mom but I sure do wish she was like Mrs. Brent. Could you help her to be more like Mrs. Brent? And help her to—to love me." Her voice broke. She cleared her throat and prayed a little longer, then blew her nose and wiped away every tear.

Now, she had to talk to Mom. Butterflies fluttered in her stomach and she stopped at the door. Could she walk to Mom's bedroom and tell her that she was sorry and that she loved her even if she wasn't Mrs. Brent?

She took a deep breath and opened the door. Canned laughter from the TV filled the hallway. The smell of hair spray drifted from Linda's room.

Slowly Teddy Jo walked down the carpeted hallway, then stopped outside Mom's closed door. What if Mom yelled at her and told her to go away? She shivered.

Finally she knocked on the door. Her heart hammered louder than her knock and she wondered if Mom could hear it.

"Who is it?" asked Carol sharply.

"It's me, Mom. Teddy Jo."

"What do you want?"

Teddy Jo swallowed hard. "Can I come in?"

There was silence, then, "I suppose, if you must."

Slowly Teddy Jo opened the door. Carol sat on the edge of her unmade bed with her head in her hands. Her nose and eyes were red from crying. She was still dressed in her work jeans and blouse.

"What do you want?"

"I'm sorry for making you cry, Mom."

"Yes, well, you did make me cry." Carol rubbed her forehead. "And now I have a terrible headache."

"I'm sorry."

"I'm just sorry that I'm not your precious Janet Brent."

Teddy Jo stepped closer to the bed. "Mom."

"What?"

"I love you."

Carol looked up in surprise. "No, you don't. If you did you wouldn't have said all those things. You wouldn't have screamed and acted like a crazy person."

Teddy Jo twisted her toe in the carpet. "I am sorry for that. I was mad and forgot for a minute that I don't do that anymore. I am a Christian, Mom. I want all of our family to be Christians and love God and go to church together."

"Yes, well, that would be nice, but I can't

see it happening." Carol tugged a pillow onto her lap and hugged it.

"Please don't say that!" Teddy Jo looked helplessly at her. "I won't ever get so mad again. I won't ever throw another fit. And I won't ever say such bad things to you. I do want us to be a happy and loving family."

Carol sighed. "So do I, Teddy Jo. So do I."

"Grandpa says we will. He prays for us and so do I. Jesus loves us, Mom. He wants us all to be happy."

Carol blinked back fresh tears. "You run along now, Teddy Jo. I'll talk to you later."

Teddy Jo hesitated, then walked out slowly and closed the door as quietly as she could. She stood in the hallway and a slow smile spread across her face. Someday this would be a house full of love.

The smile slowly faded. But first she'd have to settle her fight with Mrs. Sloan and with Grandpa. Could she do that?

12. The Mystery Solved

She had to do it and she knew it, but she hung back and let the hot sun burn down on her. She'd sent Paul to play with Jim until she finished this scary task. Yesterday she'd promised herself that she'd set things right with Mrs. Sloan and with Grandpa. She had to do it even if she never left Mrs. Sloan's house alive.

Honey barked at the screen door and Kandy looked out to see who was walking up the walk. Seeing Teddy Jo, she quickly opened the door and smiled. "Hi, Teddy Jo. Honey says hi too."

Teddy Jo bent down and patted Honey's head, then smiled as well as she could at Kandy. "Is your grandma home? I've got to talk to her."

"She's working, but I'll tell her you're here."

Teddy Jo stood nervously just inside the door while Kandy ran to a closed door and knocked and said that Teddy Jo was there.

Mrs. Sloan stepped out with a surprised look on her face. She was dressed in blue slacks and a white blouse with blue flowers. Her hair stood on end as if she'd been running her fingers through it. "What can I do for you this early in the day, Teddy Jo?"

Teddy Jo cleared her throat and thought about running out the door as fast as she could go. "I just wanted to say hello," she managed to say.

"How about a glass of orange juice?"

"All right."

"Want to go to the park with me?" Kandy fell into step with Teddy Jo as they followed Anna Sloan to the kitchen.

"Maybe later." Teddy Jo stopped just inside the kitchen and looked around for an escape route just in case she needed one later.

"Sit down, Teddy Jo. I needed a break anyway. My head gets so full of murder plots that it's hard to come down to earth."

Teddy Jo squealed and her face turned deathly white. She had been right all along! But how could Mrs. Sloan just stand there and admit it as if it were nothing?

"What's wrong, Teddy Jo?" Mrs. Sloan reached for Teddy Jo and she jumped back and hit the wall with a thud. "Oh, dear! What is it? You look as if you're going to faint."

"I want to go home," whispered Teddy Jo.

Kandy frowned and shook her head. Why

was Teddy Jo so scared? Why did she keep cringing away from Grandma? "You can't go home yet," said Kandy. "You look too weak to walk."

"I have to leave now." Teddy Jo tried to stop shaking, but she couldn't.

Anna took her arm and practically dragged her to the kitchen chair and pushed her down on it. "Sit there until you feel better. Here. Drink this."

She looked at it and groaned. She dare not eat or drink anything in this house. Oh, why had she ever talked to these strangers in the pink house? What would Grandpa do if she never got to see him again, never got to say she was sorry for making him mad?

"Your hands are like ice," said Mrs. Sloan, shaking her head. "What can I do to help you?"

"I want to go home." She started to get up, but Mrs. Sloan pressed her back down.

Honey padded across the floor and licked her bare leg, then sank to the floor with her head under Teddy Jo's chair.

"I'd better call your grandpa to come get you."

Teddy Jo gasped and stared in surprise. "To get me?" she squeaked.

"You certainly can't go home on your own."

"I could walk her home," said Kandy.

"She looks ill to me. I think Ed would want to make sure she's all right." Mrs. Sloan pressed the numbers of her touch tone tele-

phone and Teddy Jo just sat with her mouth
hanging open.

"Don't call him," she finally croaked out.
"We had a fight and I want to talk to him
alone."

Slowly Mrs. Sloan replaced the receiver,
then sat across the table from Teddy Jo and
Kandy. "Can you talk about it?"

She shook her head. "Can I leave now?"

"Finish your juice and then go when you feel
well enough."

She looked at the juice, then at Kandy who
was drinking hers right down. Finally Teddy Jo
picked up the glass and sipped. It tasted like
plain ordinary orange juice. She gulped down
half of it, then set down the glass and took a
deep breath. "I guess I'd better tell you."

Mrs. Sloan leaned forward. "I'm listening.
Would you like Kandy to leave the room?"

"I want to stay."

"I don't care if she stays." Teddy Jo
squirmed uncomfortably. "I guess you'll
probably laugh at me when I tell you."

"I won't laugh," said Kandy with sparkling
eyes. She just knew whatever it was, it was
going to be good.

Teddy Jo looked down at her hands, then up
at Mrs. Sloan. "I thought—that you killed
people."

"Oh!"

"Not my grandma!"

Teddy Jo sighed. "I know now that I was

102

wrong. You wouldn't do such a thing. But I heard you talking on the phone the first day we met you and you said you wanted somebody dead and I thought you were a murderer and I was scared."

Mrs. Sloan smiled gently. "Oh, Teddy Jo, you were partly right."

"I was?" Should she get up and run now before it was too late?

"I have a secret life."

Teddy Jo's eyes grew big and round and Kandy laughed under her breath. She knew about Grandma's secret life. Once Teddy Jo knew, she'd laugh, too.

Mrs. Sloan cleared her throat. "I am a writer, Teddy Jo."

"You are?"

"Yes. I write books for adults. I write murder mysteries. I never use my own name on my books because I don't want publicity."

"Her name on her books is Nelson Grand-by."

"I never heard of him."

"Many others in this town have, but none of them know that it's really me." Mrs. Sloan fingered the collar on her blouse. "It's my secret. Many adults read my books and some of them have been made into movies. If everyone knew who I was they'd take up all my time and invade my privacy."

"Does Grandpa know?"

"No. I wanted to tell him, but I was afraid

of what he'd say. Some people think it's
terrible that I write murder mysteries. But I
like it and I'm good at it."

"I wanted to tell you, but Grandma said I
couldn't," Kandy said with a grin.

"I sure won't tell anyone! I'll keep it a secret.
I won't even tell Paul."

Mrs. Sloan stood up and walked to the
window, then turned. "I would have liked to
tell your grandpa myself, but if you want to,
then go ahead. I know how close the two of you
are. I'm sure you never have secrets from each
other."

Teddy Jo rubbed her finger up and down the
glass. "I'd like to tell him, but I'll let you. He
likes you. A lot." Oh, but that had been hard
to say!

"Grandma likes him a lot, too," said Kandy,
bobbing her red head. "She likes him better
than anyone else."

"That's enough, Kandy."

Kandy ducked her head and grinned sheepishly.

A tinge of jealousy made Teddy Jo flinch,
but she pushed the feeling away. "I guess I'd
better go so I can talk to Grandpa. We kind of
had a fight yesterday."

"I'm sure you'll straighten everything out,"
said Mrs. Sloan. "I believe you are Ed's
favorite subject. He's very proud of you."

"I guess if you want to kiss him and he wants

to kiss you, it's all right," said Teddy Jo in a rush.

Mrs. Sloan laughed and her cheeks turned a bright pink. "Thank you, Teddy Jo."

"*Did* you kiss him, Grandma?"

"Yes."

Kandy clapped her hands. "I knew you loved him."

"Now, Kandy, don't get carried away."

Teddy Jo abruptly pushed her chair back. "I've gotta go."

"Let's meet at the park later," said Kandy. "We can play together. I can't stay much longer. Mom says she wants me home next week so we can shop for school clothes."

"I might see you at the park after I talk to Grandpa." He couldn't still be mad at her, could he? He'd forgive her once she apologized. He just had to.

She stopped at the door and turned. "Mrs. Sloan, I will keep your secret. I promise."

"Thank you, Teddy Jo. I appreciate that." Mrs. Sloan smiled, then leaned down and kissed Teddy Jo right on the cheek.

Teddy Jo blinked in surprise, then rushed out the door into the hot sunlight. She touched her cheek. She'd gone to the pink house with the fear that she might be killed, instead she got kissed.

She threw back her head and laughed, then ran home to call Grandpa.

13. A Talk with Grandpa

Teddy Jo stood in front of her mirror and looked at the girl with the tangled brown hair, dirty tee shirt, and scratched legs. She took a deep breath and doubled her fists. "Grandpa, I was wrong." She shook her head. "Grandpa, I want to talk to you. I am sorry for getting mad at you." She sighed. "Grandpa, could we have a serious talk?"

The door burst open and Paul almost fell into the bedroom. "Is Grandpa here?"

Teddy Jo shook her finger. "You were listening at the door!"

Paul shrugged and backed away a few steps. "But I didn't hear anything. Honest."

"Go watch TV."

"Where's Grandpa?"

"He's sure not hiding in my closet. Get out of my room right now!"

Paul trembled. He wanted to turn and run,

but he stood still and lifted his chin high. "You quit bossing me around!"

Her mouth dropped open and she stared in surprise at him.

"I am not gonna be a chicken any longer. You can't boss me around and Linda can't. If you want me to do something, then you ask me nice and I'll think about doing it."

"Boy, do you think you're big!"

"I am not a baby any longer!" His voice almost shook. "I'll get out of your room now." He walked out and shut the door, then tore off for the bathroom.

Teddy Jo slowly walked to her door. She sure had bossed Paul around too much and she sure had thought he was a big chicken. But no longer. He wasn't a baby. Soon he'd quit wetting his bed and everything.

In the kitchen she picked up the phone to call Grandpa. Her hand shook and she almost dropped the phone. She could do it! She'd had the courage to talk to Mrs. Sloan a while ago, so she could talk to Grandpa without falling into little pieces.

She dialed the number and waited. The phone rang and rang. She counted ten rings and hung up. Maybe Grandpa was sitting beside his phone and saying, "Well, that's Teddy Jo calling to yell at me again, so I just won't answer it."

"Who're you calling?" asked Paul from the

108

kitchen doorway. He was loudly chewing a big wad of bubble gum.

"Grandpa."

"He's not home."

"How do you know?"

"I just do." Paul blew a big bubble and it popped over his face. He peeled it loose and crammed it back into his mouth.

"I sure need to talk to him." Teddy Jo looked out the window. Mrs. Brent was weeding her flowers. She looked up and saw Teddy Jo and waved. Teddy Jo waved back.

The front doorbell rang and Paul dashed to answer it. Someday the front doorbell would ring and a man would stand there with a puppy in his arms and he'd say, "This is for Paul Miller. Do you know Paul Miller?"

He'd say he was Paul Miller, then he'd take the puppy and hold it and kiss it and put it down only when he had to.

He opened the door. "Grandpa!"

"Hi, Paul." Grandpa stepped inside, then lifted Paul high and gave him a bear hug. "How are you today?"

"I'm big and strong."

"Good for you."

Teddy Jo stood in the living room and watched them. She wanted to run to Grandpa, but she couldn't until she found out if he was still mad at her. He finally looked at her, but he didn't speak.

"Hi, Grandpa," she said weakly.

"Hello."

"Sit down if you want. Should I fix you a cup of coffee?"

"Not right now, thanks."

She looked at Paul and he caught her look and stopped dancing around Grandpa. Why was she looking at him that way? He hadn't done anything wrong, had he?

"Paul, I want to talk to Grandpa alone for a while. Will you go out and play until I call you?"

"I want to stay here." He plopped down on the couch and crossed his thin arms across his thin chest. No way would he leave unless he wanted to.

"Get out of here right now, Paul!" She stepped toward him and he jumped up and ran to the door.

"Thanks, Paul," said Grandpa. "Later you and I will have a long talk all alone."

Paul opened the door and walked out, then sat on the front step with his head in his hands. He sure wasn't as brave and strong as he'd thought. But he wouldn't always be littler than Teddy Jo. Some day he'd be as big as Grandpa and then she couldn't boss him around.

Teddy Jo chewed on her bottom lip as she slowly sank to the edge of Mom's chair. Grandpa sat on the couch with his large hands on his knees. She knew he was waiting for her to speak. She swallowed hard.

110

"Grandpa, I was wrong."

"Yes, you were."

"Mrs. Sloan is a nice lady and if you want to be friends with her, then it's all right with me. She is nice and she's not bad."

"Never eavesdrop on a private conversation, Teddy Jo. It may lead to trouble."

"I guess so."

"I know so. Anna is wonderful. I care a lot for her." He sighed. "I can't talk to you when you're over there, Teddy Jo. Come sit beside me and we'll talk."

She leaped at him and hugged him tight. "I am sure sorry, Grandpa. I love you."

He hugged her, then held her back. "You are my very own Teddy Bear Jo. You never have to be afraid that another person will come between you and me."

"Not even if you love that person?"

He grinned. "Not even then."

She rubbed the front of his tan shirt. "Do you love Mrs. Sloan?"

He was quiet for a long time. "Yes. Yes, I believe I do."

"Would you . . . marry her?"

He patted Teddy Jo's shoulder. "I might. If I do, I'll still have room in my life for you. I have a lot of love to give. I can love your mom and dad and Linda and Paul and you. I can love Anna Sloan."

"She kissed me," said Teddy Jo. "Right here."

111

He looked closely. "So she did."

Teddy Jo laughed. "Oh, Grandpa."

He cleared his throat. "I have to tell you something now that I'm ashamed to have to say."

She moved closer to him.

"I had my own suspicions of Anna Sloan and when you told me yours, it upset me because it made me more suspicious. I had no right to get angry at you. I should have sat down quietly and discussed your fears and helped you to settle them. Please forgive me."

"Oh, Grandpa." She kissed his leathery cheek.

"I decided I needed to have a talk with Anna and get some questions of mine cleared up. So I went over just a few minutes ago. She told me that you'd been there and she told me her secret. She said she told you, too."

"I sure was embarrassed."

Grandpa chuckled. "So was I. I knew there was a part of her life that she kept a secret, but I never imagined that she was a writer. I'm proud of her. I told her that."

"And did she kiss your cheek?"

"No. But I made a date to take her out for supper tonight. Kandy is going to come over here to stay with you until we get back."

"Good. And Honey, too?"

"Yes, but she'll have to stay outdoors. You know what your mother thinks of dogs in the house."

112

Teddy Jo leaned her head against Grandpa's arm. "Grandpa, I don't want to get mad at you again ever! And I don't ever want you to get mad at me. It hurts too much."

"I know. It hurt me so much I couldn't sleep last night."

"I love you, Grandpa." Suddenly she remembered Paul and she ran to the door. "You can come in now, Paul. Grandpa and I had our talk. Now it's your turn."

Paul ran past her and landed on the couch with a bounce.

Teddy Jo sat on the front step with her head in her hands and a proud smile on her lips. Grandpa had enough love for her and everyone else. She could share him with Paul and even with Anna Sloan. Her blue eyes sparkled. It sure was getting easier to be nice. One of these days she'd be just as nice as Grandpa. Even Mom would notice and maybe then she'd love her.

14. A New Carol

Teddy Jo pulled on a tee shirt that wasn't stained, dirty, or ripped. And that had been hard to find. She frowned down at herself. Did she look good enough to go shopping with Mrs. Brent? Linda had said that she'd better dress right or she'd make her stay home. She rubbed her hands down her jeans. Would that little smear of grass stain count? Linda sure was picky. Who was going to look at her and her clothes anyway?

She grabbed the five dollars that Grandpa had given her when she'd told him that she was going shopping and pushed it deep into her pocket. No way would a pickpocket get it.

The door opened and Linda poked her head in. "Are you ready, Teddy Jo? It's almost time to go. Brush your hair fast and come on!"

"I already brushed my hair."

"Well, brush it again."

Teddy Jo rolled her eyes and picked up her

brush and pulled it through her hair. She dropped it back on her dresser with a clatter, then ran after Linda to wait in the kitchen for Mrs. Brent to walk out of her house.

Paul gulped down a glass of milk, then rubbed his hand across his mouth. "Can I go to Jim's right now?"

"Go ahead," said Linda. "But you come home when we get back or when Mom and Dad get here."

"I will." He dashed through the living room and out the front door.

"There's Mrs. Brent." Linda tucked her shirt in neater and patted her hair in place. "Let's go, Teddy Jo."

Several minutes later Teddy Jo walked through the Woodland Mall beside Jane Brent and Linda. The five dollars in her pocket burned against her leg and she couldn't wait to spend it. Voices echoed around her. She stopped at the bronze elephant and rubbed her hand over it. She wanted to climb on it but Linda frowned at her and she didn't dare. She looked longingly at Circus World but Mrs. Brent had said that she needed to go to the Children's Place to see about the shirts on sale.

Teddy Jo found a tee shirt with Kermit on it and she almost bought it, but changed her mind. Even at the sale price it would've taken all her money and she wanted to buy lots of things.

They stopped in Kresge's and Teddy Jo

116

headed for the toy department. She could buy
a lot of things for five dollars. She looked past
the toys to the pictures and mirrors hanging
on the wall and suddenly she knew she wanted
to buy a gift for Mom. She'd never bought
anything for Mom before. She laughed softly
and practically danced down the aisle as she
looked at everything. And then she saw just
what she wanted. She stood in front of the
small picture and studied it carefully. It was a
still life of flowers sitting on a wooden table.
It was marked down and she had just enough
money. She carefully lifted the picture down
and walked to the check-out. Wouldn't Mom
be surprised? She could hang it in her bedroom
and look at it every day.

Teddy Jo waited while the woman ahead of
her paid for a pack of batteries and two beach
towels. She couldn't wait to see Mom's face
when she saw her gift.

Teddy Jo looked at the picture again and her
heart sank. She liked the picture and she'd
love to hang it in her bedroom, but Mom
wouldn't. Art wasn't that important to Mom.
Teddy Jo frowned. Maybe it was only her artwork that Mom didn't like. Mom had pictures
hanging in the living room and hallway and her
bedroom.

"Can I help you, little girl?" asked the clerk.

Teddy Jo stepped forward and handed the
picture to the woman. "I'm buying this for my
mom."

"Oh." She rang up the sale and held her hand out for the money.

"I think she'll like it."

"It's very pretty." The clerk stuck the picture in a bag and stapled it shut.

Teddy Jo walked out of line and waited near the gumball machine for Linda and Mrs. Brent.

For two more hours she walked through the mall with Linda and Mrs. Brent. It sure got boring looking at clothes and shoes and things, but she didn't complain once. She was proud of herself for walking along with a smile on her face. Once she'd let out a tired sigh, but they hadn't heard.

At home Teddy Jo changed into shorts and a suntop with straps that tied at the back of her neck. Soon Mom would be home and she'd give her the picture and watch the glad expression on her face.

Grandpa drove in just after Carol and Larry. Teddy Jo waited at the front window, the picture clutched tightly in her hands. Linda was still at the Brents and Paul hadn't come home yet.

Teddy Jo watched Dad stop and talk with Grandpa as Mom walked to the front door. Teddy Jo opened the door wide and smiled and said, "Hi, Mom. I've got something for you."

Carol stopped near the couch. "You have?"

"I wanted to buy you a gift today, so I did."

Teddy Jo handed the bag with the picture inside to Carol. "I wish I could have wrapped it but I didn't have any pretty paper."

"What did you buy for yourself?"

"Nothing. I wanted to get something for you." Oh, why didn't she open the bag and pull out the picture? Teddy Jo's stomach fluttered and she could barely stand still.

Carol slowly pulled the picture out and looked at it, then looked at Teddy Jo. "Did you think of this on your own?"

"Yes." Why was Mom acting so funny? "Is it all right?"

Giant tears welled up in Carol's eyes. "Thank you, Teddy Jo. You never did anything like this for me. The picture is beautiful and it will look good in my bedroom."

Teddy Jo thought her heart would burst with happiness. "I'm glad you're my mom."

"You are?"

Grandpa and Larry walked in and Carol turned with the picture and showed it to them.

"I'll hang it for you," said Larry, taking it from her.

"It is beautiful," said Grandpa. "You have a good eye for art, Teddy Jo."

"Thanks." She caught Grandpa's hand and held it tightly so that she wouldn't float up, up, and away.

Larry walked off, saying he had to find a hammer and a nail.

"Come to the kitchen and I'll make coffee," said Carol, leading the way.

She filled the teakettle with water and put it on to boil, then turned to look at Grandpa and Teddy Jo. "I can't get over the change in you, Teddy Jo."

"I'm happy, too, Mom," said Teddy Jo, beaming proudly.

"You'll have to get used to a happy, loving family, Carol," said Grandpa as he sat at the table. "And it's going to get better and better."

Carol sank to a chair and locked her hands together on the table. "I want it to get better, but how can it when I'm the way I am?"

"I love you, Mom," said Teddy Jo from where she stood near the sink.

"How can you? I'm not a very good mother."

"You can learn to be," said Grandpa softly.

Teddy Jo came over and stood close to Carol and slipped an arm around her shoulders. "Jesus can help you just like he helps me."

"Maybe you're right, Teddy Jo."

"I am right! We can be a happy Christian family, can't we, Grandpa? Jesus can help Mom, can't he, Grandpa?"

Grandpa reached across the table and patted Carol's hands. "Carol, I've been praying for you—for this family—for a long time. Jesus does make a difference and you can see that in me and in Teddy Jo. If you let Jesus into your life, he'll change you, too."

Carol looked at Teddy Jo, then at Grandpa. "I do want that."

"Pray with Mom, Grandpa, just like you prayed with me and Paul."

"Is that what you want, Carol?"

Carol sniffed, then nodded.

Grandpa told her why Jesus had come to die on the cross for all people and that he'd risen and gone to heaven where he always watched over his own. Then he prayed with her while Teddy Jo stood beside Mom with her head bowed and her heart leaping for joy.

"We have a brand new mom in the Miller home," said Grandpa.

"I am a Christian now," said Mom in awe. "Jesus is my own Savior."

Teddy Jo looked at Mom for a long time. She didn't look any different, but Teddy Jo knew that God had given her a new spirit. Grandpa had showed her in the Bible where it said that the person who accepted Jesus was now a new creature in Christ, a whole new person inside.

"Why are you looking at me, Teddy Jo?" asked Carol suspiciously.

"I like to look at you. You're the prettiest mom in the whole world!"

"Oh, Teddy Jo!" Carol flushed, then smiled. "Thank you."

Teddy Jo threw her arms around Carol and hugged her. Carol stiffened, then finally slipped her arms around Teddy Jo. She rubbed her hands up and down Teddy Jo's thin back.

"I love you, Theodora Josephine."

Teddy Jo looked at her in surprise and Carol reached up and kissed Teddy Jo's cheek. Gingerly Teddy Jo touched the kiss, her eyes wide. Mom had kissed her! Mom had said she loved her!

"This is a happy day," said Grandpa.

"A perfect day," said Teddy Jo. She laughed happily, then kissed Mom's soft pink cheek.

If you enjoyed the Teddy Jo series,
double your fun with the Tyler Twins!

The Tyler Twins series is available at your local bookstore, or you may order by mail (U.S. and territories only). Send your check or money order plus $.75 per book ordered for postage and handling to:

Tyndale D.M.S.
Box 80
Wheaton, IL 60189

Prices subject to change.
Allow 4-6 weeks for delivery.

Tyndale House Publishers, Inc.